Ready to go . . .

Eddy sat down on the high seat and clutched the handlebar grips with both hands. The bicycle was trembling as if it were ready to go. The headlight made a wobbling blob of light like a jewel on the wall of the coat closet. The telephone was ringing in the front hall, and the bicycle wheels made a whirring noise as they began to turn, and there was a softer sound, too—what was that?—like the murmur of waves rolling up on a sandy beach.

But the bike did not take him to the seashore—it took him to the Emerson Park Playground in the very middle of the town of Concord, Massachusetts, and to the Saturday-afternoon baseball game, just the way he wanted it to.

But at the last minute he caught a glimpse of something in the little round mirror on the handlebars, a pair of staring eyes. They were not Eddy's. Whose were they?

THE HALL FAMILY CHRONICLES

◆

The Time Bike

JANE LANGTON

The Hall Family Chronicles

HarperTrophy®
An Imprint of HarperCollinsPublishers

Harper Trophy® is a registered trademark
of HarperCollins Publishers Inc.

The Time Bike
Text copyright © 2000 by Jane Langton
Illustrations copyright © 2000 by Erik Blegvad
Printed in the United States of America. For information
address HarperCollins Children's Books, a division of HarperCollins
Publishers, 1350 Avenue of the Americas, New York, NY 10019.

Library of Congress Cataloging-in-Publication Data
Langton, Jane.
    The time bike / by Jane Langton.
        p.   cm
    Summary: Eddy Hall receives a mysterious gift from India, an old-
fashioned bike that transports its rider through time.
        ISBN 0-06-028437-4 — ISBN 0-06-028438-2 (lib. bdg.)
        ISBN 0-06-440792-6 (pbk.)
        [1. Time travel—Fiction.   2. Bicycles and bicycling—Fiction.]   I. Title.
PZ7.L2717Ti   2000   99-39896
[Fic]—dc21   CIP
                                                                       AC

Typography by Larissa Lawrynenko
First Harper Trophy edition, 2002
❖
Visit us on the World Wide Web!
www.harperchildrens.com

For Gabriel and Colin

CONTENTS

Time is but the stream I go a-fishing in.

-HENRY THOREAU

The
Time Bike

I

GOOD DAY, BAD DAY

*I*T WAS EDDY'S BIRTHDAY, so of course it should have
been a good day.

And for Eddy it *was* a good day, because his birthday present was a bicycle, a new Timuri bike in Killer
Tomato Red with rock shocks and compression damping
and rear derailleur and rapid-fire shifters and twenty-one
combinations of gears that worked with handlebar grips.

It was the bike he had hardly dared hope for, it was
so expensive. But Uncle Freddy and Aunt Alex had
found the money somewhere. When Eddy came running
down in the morning, there it was in the front hall, shiny
and red and beautiful.

He took it out before breakfast and raced up Walden

Street to the center of Concord, whizzed around the corner of Main Street to the library, veered left on Sudbury Road, and sped home by way of Stow Street and Everett.

All the way around he hoped to see admiring glances from the sidewalk, but the only person who noticed him was his old friend Oliver Winslow. Oliver saw Eddy on his new bike and whistled through his teeth.

But of course there was another reason why it was a good day. The other reason began in the middle of the afternoon, when the telephone rang.

Aunt Alex had been waiting and waiting. Her voice trembled as she said, "Hello?" And then she gasped, "Oh, thank you, thank you. I'm so glad."

And then she dropped the phone because Uncle Freddy himself was walking in the front door.

Aunt Alex threw her arms around him. "You won, you won!"

Uncle Freddy beamed and kissed her and said, "Well, as a matter of fact, I guess I did."

Eddy ran in from the back porch, where he had been tinkering with his bike. "You won, Uncle Freddy? You beat old man Preek?" He dropped to his knees and threw up his arms. "Bow down, ye nations! Bow down before Selectman Frederick Hall!"

"Oh, Eddy, don't be stupid," said Eleanor, clattering

down the stairs. But she was grinning too. "Oh, Uncle Freddy, congratulations."

It was true. Uncle Freddy had beaten the other candidate for the office of Concord selectman. He would now be a member of the board that ran the town.

But it had been a fierce and nasty campaign. His opponent, Ralph Preek, had accused Uncle Freddy of everything awful.

The most dangerous was that he wouldn't know how to handle the town budget of forty million dollars, whereas *he*, Ralph Q. Preek, was the manager of a bank and an expert on financial affairs.

Mr. Preek's attacks had not worked. Yesterday most of the voters had gone quietly into the Hunt Gym and all the other Concord voting places and chosen Frederick Hall as their new selectman.

"Oh, Fred, I'm so glad," said Aunt Alex, her eyes wet with tears.

But then Uncle Freddy's smile faded, and he said solemnly, "He won't forgive me, you know. He'll get back at us somehow, just wait and see."

"But what could he possibly do?" said Aunt Alex.

"I don't know. He'll think of something."

The bad thing didn't happen until everyone in the house was sound asleep.

2

STOLEN!

*E*DDY'S NEW BIRTHDAY bike was gone.

Horrified, he stared around the front porch. Last night he had left it leaning against the railing. This morning it wasn't there.

There was nothing on the porch but the electric lawn mower with its coil of orange cable and a bag of chicken feed and a bamboo rake with missing teeth.

Eddy's new Timuri bike with rock shocks and compression damping and rear derailleur and rapid-fire shifters and twenty-one combinations of gears was gone, all gone.

He went rampaging through the house, looking for Aunt Alex and Uncle Freddy. Or Eleanor! Maybe

Eleanor had taken it. He wouldn't put it past her.

Nobody was in the house. Eddy stormed out the rear door to the back porch and saw Aunt Alex feeding her chickens, scattering cracked corn around their fenced-in yard. They were Black Rosecomb bantams with many-colored feathers. The rooster stalked around among the hens, sticking out his shining black chest and arching his green tail.

"Aunt Alex," began Eddy angrily, but the jaunty little rooster chose that moment to lift his head and shout, *"ARK-ARK-ARK-AROOOOOO."*

"Aunt Alex!"

Looking up at his furious face, Aunt Alex stopped scattering corn and unrolled the chicken-wire gate. "Eddy, dear, what is it?"

"My bike! Have you seen my bike?"

"Oh, dear." Aunt Alex followed Eddy back through the house to the front porch, and together they stared at the place where last night there had been a bicycle, where now there was only a railing with a lot of lathe-turned spindles.

Eddy glowered at the bubbles of paint on the top of the railing, the bubbles he had so often flattened with his thumb. "You see?" he said, his voice choked with tears. "Somebody stole it right off the porch."

"Hey, guess what." Eddy's sister Eleanor burst out

the front door, ready for school. "Amanda Upshaw is giving a party. With invitations and a real live band."

They looked at her dolefully. "Eleanor, dear," said Aunt Alex, "do you know what's happened to Eddy's new bike? It was right here on the porch last night, and now it's gone."

"Uh-oh," said Eleanor. "Did you lock it to the railing?"

"No," said Eddy hotly. "I mean, a person ought to be able to leave his bike on his own front porch."

"Well, then, you see? It's your own fault." Eleanor flounced down the porch steps, then ran back up to look in the mailbox in case her party invitation had already come, but it hadn't, so she ran down again and turned right on the sidewalk, heading for the Concord-Carlisle High School.

Eleanor didn't need a bike, because her school was in walking distance. But Eddy's middle school was miles away on the other side of town. "I'll have to walk," he said crossly. "I've already missed the bus."

"I'll drive you, Eddy dear," said Aunt Alex.

Grumpily, Eddy climbed into the car. On the way to school he couldn't stop mumbling, "My bike, my brand-new bike."

Then he had an idea. He turned to Aunt Alex as she stopped the car at a traffic light. "Can't Uncle Freddy do

6

something? I mean, now that he's a selectman?"

She glanced at him doubtfully. "What exactly would you want him to do, Eddy?"

"Call up the police chief," said Eddy angrily. "Demand a house-to-house search."

The light changed. Aunt Alex sped forward in the direction of the Sanborn School. "Oh, Eddy, your uncle isn't in charge of the police department. He can't tell them what to do."

Eddy sank back and stared at the cars whizzing by the other way. His bike was gone, his brand-new bike!

Aunt Alex was a quiet woman, a little shy. But now, as the car pulled up in front of Eddy's school, she said a brave thing. "I'll call them, Eddy. I'll call them myself."

While Eddy was climbing glumly out of the car, hitching up his backpack, and walking into the Sanborn School, the president of the Thoreau Street Bank sat in his office, shuffling the papers on his desk.

The president was the defeated candidate for selectman, Ralph Q. Preek.

Mr. Preek hated losing. He especially hated losing to his old enemy, Frederick Hall.

Their dislike for each other went back a long way. There had been a number of insults.

One was *The Affair of the Goose*, as Mr. Preek liked

to call it. A tender part of his anatomy still bore the scar.

Another was his bitter disappointment when the Thoreau Street Bank had nearly, *very nearly*, taken over the Halls' shabby house for unpaid taxes. But somehow or other those careless people had come up with the money.

Mr. Preek ground his teeth, remembering, and clenched his fists. There must be *something* he could do to take revenge. He began pulling open his file drawers and slamming them shut, *CRASH, CRASH!*

He couldn't find what he was looking for. He put his head out of his office door and called his secretary. "Letitia, do we still have records going back to the bank's early days? You know, fifty or sixty years ago?"

"Up-attic," said Letitia crisply. She led the way to a steep little back staircase that he had never seen before. "Follow me," she said, pointing gallantly upward. She bounced up the stairs, followed slowly by Mr. Preek, who could only gasp his way up from step to step. Then she left him there, pawing through heaps of yellowed paper powdered with plaster dust and chewed at the edges by rats.

Mr. Preek spent an hour on his knees in the attic, tossing old papers this way and that. At last he found one that interested him. He lumbered downstairs, carried it to his desk, and telephoned an old friend, Miss Madeline Prawn.

"Madeline?"

"Oh, Ralph, is it really you?"

"It is indeed, and I've just found something that I think will interest you."

No, it was not the fault of Ralph Q. Preek that Eddy's new bike had disappeared. Mr. Preek had nothing to do with it. But something else had blossomed in his mind, something worse. Worse not just for Eddy, but for Eleanor and Aunt Alex and Uncle Freddy, and even for the cats stretched out under Aunt Alex's kitchen table, sound asleep.

Worse—it was very much worse. A hundred times worse than a stolen bike.

3

THE CRATE

OF COURSE AUNT ALEX called the police about Eddy's bike, but they were discouraging. When she tried to describe it, all she could say was, "It's red, I think, with a lot of gears."

"Oh, well," said the officer on the phone, "there's a thousand other bikes like that in Concord. Tell the boy to keep his eyes open. I suppose he'd recognize it if he saw another kid with his bike?"

"Well, the trouble is," said Aunt Alex, "it was brand-new. There wasn't a scratch on it."

"Too bad," said the officer. "I'm really sorry, but I'm afraid there's no way we can help."

So Eddy had to get used to the fact that from now on

he would be without a bicycle. Aunt Alex and Uncle Freddy had spent a lot of money on his birthday bike, he knew that, and they couldn't just go out and buy another one. It was true that Uncle Freddy had become a selectman, but that was no help. Selectmen worked for nothing.

So Eddy was a good sport. When Bus 8 stopped at the corner next morning, he climbed on without complaint. After all, it was June. There were only a couple more weeks of school.

"Hey, Eddy," hooted Billy Porter, one of the sixth graders, "where's your bike? Why aren't you riding your new bike to school?"

Eddy laughed and made a joke. "I missed you, that's why. I missed all my tiny little friends."

And they laughed, because Eddy was always so funny.

When Eddy had walked into the Sanborn School on the first day of eighth grade, way last fall, a new burst of funny talk had begun gushing out of him.

And of course it wasn't just talk. Aunt Alex and Uncle Freddy were amazed by the way he had shot up in the last six months. His skinny arms ended in big hands and his long legs in big feet. He was as tall as Uncle Freddy. His red hair had grown too. It flopped over his eyes, and he had to keep throwing it back.

"Your hair," said Aunt Alex one day, "don't you think, Eddy—?" But he interrupted her at once. "Oh, yes, I think all the time. I think the world is round, I think the sky is blue, I think you are my aunt, I think I am your nephew, I think my hair is ab-so-lute-ly perfect."

So Aunt Alex smiled and said no more, because there was no way of arguing with Eddy. He could outtalk you every time. He never stopped. Words poured out of him, cheerful, giddy words, except when they were bloodthirsty and disgusting. Once he found a book about farm animals and read it aloud at the supper table—how to give an enema to a cow or slaughter a pig.

His social studies teacher called Uncle Freddy one day to ask a strange question. "Mr. Hall, I've been wondering. Could you tell me, is everything all right at home?"

Uncle Freddy was baffled. "All right at home?"

"Well, I just thought I'd call you," said Miss Brisket. "Edward has a tendency to keep telling jokes all day. I mean, the trouble is, he keeps the other children in stitches. It makes it so difficult for me to impart knowledge to my class. I thought perhaps he might be covering up some inner depression. You know, deep down inside."

"I see," said Uncle Freddy. "You mean he's so sad he

12

has to make people laugh? If he were happy, would he make them cry?"

There was a pause. Then the teacher said coldly, "Mr. Hall, it is clear that you are in a state of denial."

"Well, I'm sorry," said Uncle Freddy, and he promised to speak to Eddy. As he put down the phone, he couldn't help wondering if the knowledge the teacher imparted was as important as Eddy's jokes, but of course that was a terrible way to look at it.

He took Eddy aside and urged him to keep quiet in school. "For heaven's sake, Eddy, think of the poor teacher. You're not letting her do her job."

"Well, all right," said Eddy. And after that he raised his hand whenever he wanted to ask a question. But his questions were worse than his jokes. Sometimes Miss Brisket had no answer. The poor woman knew (somewhere deep down inside) that Eddy was smarter than she was, but she remained in a state of denial.

It was clear to Uncle Freddy what was happening. It was perfectly simple. His nephew Eddy was surging out of childhood, that was all. His jokes weren't some upside-down way of being miserable; they were the joyful explosion of a greedy interest in everything, everything in the whole world. The result was an eruption of words in a never-ending stream.

But when the doorbell rang a few days after his bike

was stolen, Eddy was not at home to fill the air with funny talk and excited questions.

"What is it?" said Aunt Alex, opening the front door.

"A crate, madam. We wish to deliver a crate to"—the deliveryman looked at the paper in his hand—"Mr. Edward Hall."

Miss Madeline Prawn, who had once lived next door to the Halls and had then moved away, to their intense relief, was delighted by Ralph Preek's hints about a wondrous possibility. He kept calling her with questions and suggestions.

"My great-uncle? Why of course, Ralph, I was deeply attached to beloved Great-Uncle—uh—I've forgotten his name for the moment, but do tell me, Ralph, do you really mean that he—"

"I think so, Madeline. Indeed, I am almost certain of it. Wasn't your great-uncle's name Peregrine Pontius Prawn?"

There was a short pause, and then Miss Prawn gushed, "Why, of course! Darling Great-Uncle Peregrine! How could I forget?"

"Well, I'm sending a letter to Frederick Hall, warning him of eventualities that may ensue."

"Eventualities?"

"A court order requiring him to evacuate the premises."

"Evacuate the premises?"

"Leave. Get out. Buzz off. Do I make myself clear?"

Miss Prawn giggled wildly and said, "Perfectly!"

4

THE GIFT FROM INDIA

A SMALL, ODD-LOOKING TRUCK was parked in the driveway. On the side it said "*Transcendental Transport.*" The deliveryman looked a little strange too. He wore a pink turban on his head. His face was dark, his eyes bright.

For a panicky moment Aunt Alex wondered if Eddy had ordered something expensive from one of his crazy catalogues. "Is there a return address?"

"It comes from India. Where shall we put it?"

"Oh," said Aunt Alex, flustered, "bring it in here, right here in the front hall."

"Yes, of course." The man in the pink turban glanced

past her into the house and smiled, as if he recognized the stairway and the plaster bust and the bronze statue on the newel post and the umbrella stand and the telephone desk and the two cross-eyed cats nestled under the desk—as if he had known them since the beginning of time.

"Very well," he said. He turned away and went to the truck, where another deliveryman was opening the door in the back. The second man wore a turban too, the color of a robin's egg.

Aunt Alex watched as they lifted out a long, narrow crate and carried it up the porch steps. She held the screen door wide so that they could bring the crate inside and set it down at the foot of the stairs. One of the cats slipped out the door as the crate came in.

The man in the pink turban smiled as he handed Aunt Alex a piece of paper. "Sign here, please."

Aunt Alex signed, and the men went away. But no sooner had she closed the door than she jerked it open again. There were so many questions she wanted to ask. *Oh, tell me, please tell me, who sent it? Who are you? Won't you come in?*

But they had vanished. *They must have made a jackrabbit start,* thought Aunt Alex. She went to the basement for a crowbar and brought it up and laid it on

17

the crate, so that Eddy could pry the nails loose and pull away the boards. He wouldn't be home from school for hours yet.

Then she sat down at the telephone desk to write a letter to her daughter, Georgie. Georgie was the youngest of the three kids who lived at No. 40 Walden Street. Her school had finished early, and she had gone away with her best friend, Frieda, to spend a few weeks with Frieda's family at Squam Lake.

Aunt Alex picked up her pen to begin her letter, thinking of the way Georgie had beamed at her from the car window as she waved good-bye. How she would miss her!

Then Aunt Alex laughed and looked up at the clock on the wall, because it was announcing the wrong time, just as usual—*"Cuckoo, cuckoo, cuckoo!"* The correct time was twelve o'clock, of course, not three.

She watched as the cuckoo jumped back inside and slapped against the little door, which banged shut and fell off.

Aunt Alex picked it up. How typical of Miss Prawn's farewell present. The cuckoo clock was a gift from an awful neighbor who had luckily moved away. It was not made of hand-carved wood like a clock made in Switzerland. It was plastic, with a plastic cuckoo and battery-driven plastic works. Eddy had once tried to fix it, but afterward the clock was more wrong than ever.

Patiently Aunt Alex sat at the desk writing her letter, a thin figure crouched in a narrow cone of light within the shadowy darkness of the front hall of the house.

Around her the large room opened its haunted spaces.

The whole house, Aunt Alex knew, was a little mysterious. In the first place it didn't look like the rest of the houses in the town of Concord. They were sensible square white-painted buildings with green shutters. The Halls' house had a tower with a bulging dome, and it was wrapped in porches. One of the porches had a huge round opening in the lattice like a moon gate in an oriental garden.

Both inside and out, the house had a feeling of eerie playfulness. It was as though some sort of sparkling powder had been mixed with the cement of the foundation, or a spell had been banged into the timbers with a hammer, or a gauzy veil of enchantment had been stretched over the roof beams under the shingles.

Even the six cats in the house were not like other people's cats, because their orange spots were absolutely identical, and even their crossed eyes were exactly the same.

The cats were part of the general strangeness of No. 40 Walden Street. One never knew what might happen

19

anywhere in the house, in the kitchen or the attic, in the parlor or the schoolroom or the front hall.

Especially in the front hall. The front hall was a crossing place, not just between upstairs and downstairs, or kitchen and parlor, or front door and back door.

The white plaster bust of Henry Thoreau, for instance, was an intersection of strange forces. Henry stood on a tall stand, gazing with his plaster eyes in the direction of Walden Pond. The real Henry had been dead for a long time, but his books were very much alive in the house at No. 40 Walden Street.

To Aunt Alex and Uncle Freddy they were treasures. They taught about them in a school, their very own school in this very house.

But of course it wasn't just the bust of Henry that was a crossing place. The tall woman on the newel post was another. Like the ladies of the Concord Grange she had a ribbon across her chest. It said "TRUTH" in big bronze letters. There were dusky stains like pictures on her metal skirts, dark images of things—a church and a balloon, fishes and cats, a jewel with coppery rays.

Eddy and Eleanor called the tall metal lady "Mrs. Truth," because she looked so motherly and kind. One of her arms was lifted high to hold a star-shaped lamp— the light of truth, guessed Aunt Alex—but the light had burned out, leaving the hall gloomy and dark.

"It needs a new bulb, I think," Aunt Alex had said, but Eddy had insisted, "No, no, it's the wiring." And then he tried to fix it, but suddenly it went *ZAP!* and after that it never worked again.

Aunt Alex finished her letter, then lifted her head in surprise. One of the cats was meowing and clawing at the screen door, and she could hear the burbling sound of her flock of chickens in the backyard. But there was another soft murmur right here in the front hall. Turning her head, she saw that it came from the crate that was waiting for Eddy.

She got up and put her ear against the crate, but the sound died away and was gone.

5

DISAPPOINTMENT

*E*DDY GAZED AT THE crate. He was thrilled. It was a bicycle. It had to be a bicycle. The shape of the box was just right for a bike, a new bike to replace the one that had been stolen.

As he pried up the boards with the crowbar and the nails shrieked loose, he grew more and more excited. It was a wonderful new bike from halfway around the world.

It was a bicycle, all right. As the boards fell away and he tore off the newspaper wrapping, it stood revealed, brand-new and entirely his own.

He was dismayed. "Oh," he said, "it's not . . ."

It was an old-fashioned bicycle, the kind you ride sitting upright. Everything about it was out of date. It had high handlebars and a wicker basket and a speedometer and fat tires and a mirror and shiny fenders and a chain guard. Instead of twenty-one speeds, there was only one. And of course there were no shock absorbers, only a silly pair of springs under the seat.

Eddy hated the bike at sight. He didn't know what to say.

"Is there a card to tell who it's from?" said Uncle Freddy, pretending not to notice Eddy's crestfallen face.

"Yes," said Aunt Alex cheerfully. "Look, Eddy, there's a tag on the handlebars."

Slowly Eddy reached for it. "It says, 'Srinagar, Kashmir.'"

"Oh, of course," said Uncle Freddy. "It's a present from Krishna. You remember Prince Krishna, Edward?"

"Oh, right," said Eddy, his voice hollow. He remembered Prince Krishna very well. Prince Krishna was married to Uncle Freddy's sister Lily. He had sent them presents before, wonderful presents, presents a million times better than this, presents that did weird and wonderful things, like the diamond in the attic window and the astonishing stereoscope and the swing in the summerhouse and the fragile old American flag. It was too bad Prince Krishna didn't know anything about bicycles. "I suppose I have to write him a thank-you letter, right?"

"You certainly do," said Aunt Alex, remembering an astonishing meeting with Prince Krishna in the past, right here in this very front hall. Now she understood why the deliveryman had smiled when he saw the front hall. He must have been a friend of Krishna's.

Eddy looked gloomily at the bike. Not only would he have to write a thank-you letter, he'd have to ride the bike once or twice to show Uncle Freddy and Aunt Alex how grateful he was.

Where could he ride it without being seen? His friends would laugh at him. Or else they'd feel sorry for him, and that would be worse.

Aunt Alex glanced at Uncle Freddy, and together they began picking up the newspapers and collecting the pieces of the crate. "Come on, Eddy," said Uncle Freddy crossly. "You can help."

Halfheartedly Eddy lent a hand, and soon the bicycle was left standing free in the hall, propped on its kickstand beside the metal lady on the newel post.

For its long journey in the crate, the pedals had been removed. Grumpily, Eddy went looking for a wrench. He turned the handlebars around. Now the stupid bike was ready to go.

Aunt Alex looked out from the schoolroom. "Aren't you going to ride it, Eddy?"

"Not now, I guess. Not right now."

"Oh," said Aunt Alex, "well, all right." She disappeared again, leaving him alone with his new bicycle from India.

He stared at it glumly. It was bad enough to have had his good bike stolen, but somehow it was worse to have had his hopes raised for another wonderful bike, and then to be so horribly disappointed.

Resentment rose in Eddy's breast. The out-of-date bike fitted right in with his out-of-date family. Just look at all the ways Uncle Freddy and Aunt Alex lived in the past! Eddy counted them on his fingers.

One, they refused to have a television set in the house. When the old one gave up for good, did Uncle Freddy buy a new one? He did not!

Two, instead of writing their papers and books on a computer, they still banged away on a noisy old typewriter.

Three—what was three? Well, look at Aunt Alex's silly chickens. Look at the way she hung up the wet laundry with clothespins.

There was a scrabbling noise from the front porch. Eddy's big sister was home from high school, looking in the mailbox. Eleanor was expecting a dumb invitation to some dumb party. She threw open the door and dumped the mail on the table.

"Anything for me?" said Eddy sweetly, just to give her a pain.

"Oh, shut up, Eddy." Then Eleanor saw the new bike. "What's that doing here?"

"It's my new bicycle," said Eddy. "You want it? You can have it. It's all yours."

"I hate riding boys' bikes," said Eleanor. "Anyway, it's out of style. I mean it's really extinct. Nobody rides a bike like that anymore."

"No kidding," said Eddy.

He was disappointed in the bicycle and Eleanor was disappointed in the mail, which was nothing but bills and a postcard of congratulation from Uncle Freddy's brother, Ned.

It just said, "HURRAY!"

There was one more envelope in the mail, but it was just a boring-looking letter from the bank for Uncle Freddy. On the corner of the envelope there was a printed return address:

> *RALPH Q. PREEK, PRESIDENT*
> *THOREAU STREET BANK*
> *CONCORD, MASSACHUSETTS*
> *01742*

There was no invitation for Eleanor from Amanda Upshaw. Eleanor sighed, feeling hurt and left out.

But out of doors Aunt Alex's bantam rooster was cock of the walk, and it crowed loudly, "*I AM THE KING OF THE HEN COOP. ARK-ARK-ARK-AROOOOOO.*"

And the cuckoo clock struck midnight at four o'clock in the afternoon.

6

THE TIME BIKE

*T*HREE DAYS WENT BY, and the bicycle from India was still in the front hall beside the stairs, in the way.

"Eddy," said Uncle Freddy, "would you move it? Why not put it on the front porch where you kept the other one? But lock it to the railing this time."

So it won't be stolen? Eddy smiled grimly. Who would steal such a dumb old bike? But even so, he didn't put it on the front porch where anybody could see it. He found a perfect hiding place for it, a shadowy triangular nook next to the coat closet under the front hall stairs.

It was just the right size, and it had a crimson velvet

curtain on a drawstring that hid his skateboard and Uncle Freddy's old golf bag and a croquet set with a couple of broken mallets.

Laboriously, Eddy carried the old stuff up to the attic. Then he wheeled his shameful new bicycle into the space behind the curtain.

In the dark it gleamed a little, the way his old rocket model had glowed in the dark because phosphorescent stuff was mixed with the plastic. His embarrassing new bicycle must be coated with phosphorescent paint.

It trembled slightly under his hands as he propped it upright, almost as if it were alive. Little sparkles flickered around the rims of the wheels. And there was a sound, a kind of whispering murmur.

Eddy pulled the curtain aside to let in light and peered at the dial mounted on the handlebars. It wasn't a speedometer—it was a clock. And there was a dome-shaped bell on top, just like the one on an old-fashioned alarm clock. The whole thing looked just like a clock in a cartoon, the kind that bounces up and down when the alarm goes off.

He looked more closely at the dial. How weird! It didn't say 1, 2, 3, 4, all the way to 12. In fact, there were two dials. The words printed on them were very small. One said:

DAYS

and the other:

YEARS

There were a great many little marks around the circle of the Days dial—probably 365 of them, decided Eddy, one for every day of the year.

The Years dial was different. It went from 0 to 10 to 100 to 1,000 to 10,000 to 100,000. A hundred thousand years! What did it mean, a clock that told the time in thousands of years?

And there was a tab at the side, some sort of on-off switch. No, it wasn't an on-off switch, it was a plus-and-minus switch. What did that mean, plus and minus?

"Why, Eddy," said Aunt Alex, suddenly appearing in the front hall with Eleanor, "what a lovely headlight. It sparkles like a diamond."

"It does?" Eddy looked. The rocket-shaped headlight on the front fender was just one more thing that was out of style. He tried to turn it off, but there was no switch.

"It reminds me of something," said Eleanor, narrowing her eyes, staring at it through her big glasses.

Eddy knew what she was thinking of—the big jewel that had once been part of the stained-glass window in the attic, that huge chunk of glass that had turned out in the end to be a diamond, a real diamond, so valuable that it was beyond price. "It's not much good without a switch," he said. "The battery will run down any minute."

"The one in back is pretty too," said Aunt Alex, bending low over the rear fender, where the red reflector shone in the light of the desk lamp. "It's like a ruby, a real ruby." She stood up and smiled at Eddy. "It's like a bicycle from fairyland."

Then she went into the kitchen with Eleanor, and Eddy went back to studying his new bicycle with more interest than before.

He climbed on the seat to see what it felt like and dropped the curtain again. Now he was alone in the dark with the bike. In front of him the headlight shone on the wall of the coat closet, making a bright pattern like a star.

To his surprise it felt good to perch erect, high above the floor. It was sort of majestic and dignified, like riding an elephant.

Something white twirled in front of him—the tag on the handlebars. Eddy reached for it, but it kept fluttering and twisting. Finally he got it between his fingers. Pulling open the curtain, he looked at the tag. One side still said *Srinagar, Kashmir*. The other said:

TIME BIKE

Time Bike! What did it mean?

He could hear Aunt Alex talking quietly from the kitchen with Eleanor, who was complaining loudly about Amanda Upshaw's party.

"I still don't have an invitation! Becky's got one. Lisa's got one. It's only me, I'm the only one that hasn't got one. I mean, they've all got invitations already, all the best kids!"

There was a pause, and then Aunt Alex said, "What do you mean by 'best kids'?"

"Oh, you know, Aunt Alex. They're—oh, I don't know. If you could see them, you'd know what I mean."

"I see," said Aunt Alex.

Eddy stopped listening. What if he set the dial of the clock for some time in the past, like six months ago? Maybe it really was a time bike. Maybe it would really take him back to last December. Dreamily, he put his fingers on the setscrew that moved the hand of the dial that counted days.

Then he came to his senses. The idea was too scary. He should think it over first and then try it very carefully. Those people in fairy stories who were given three wishes always got in trouble. They wasted all three because they didn't think. He would be more careful.

But at that instant the little rooster in the backyard crowed noisily, and the silly cuckoo popped out of the clock and squawked.

Eddy's hand jerked. The bicycle jiggled, and the bell went *ding*. There was a flash of lightning in the little round mirror on the handlebars, and a humming noise from the wheels as if they were going around.

It was only for a moment. Then the vibration stopped. The *ding*ing stopped. Eddy got off the bike and opened the curtain.

Through the oval window in the front door he could see the trees across the road, and the grass in the front yard. Everything was green. It was still June, not last December.

The bike was a failure. It didn't work. It wasn't a time bike. The strange dials didn't mean anything at all.

Aunt Alex and Eleanor were still talking in the kitchen.

"What do you mean by 'best kids'?" said Aunt Alex.

"Oh, you know, Aunt Alex. They're—oh, I don't know. If you could see them, you'd know what I mean."

"I see," said Aunt Alex.

7

FISHING IN THE STREAM OF TIME

*T*HEY SAT AT THE KITCHEN table eating Aunt Alex's spaghetti.

Aunt Alex was not a natural-born cook. Her cakes were often black on the bottom, and the gravy in her stews sometimes boiled away. It wasn't that she was careless; she was just busy.

Aunt Alex and Uncle Freddy were teachers in their school, the Concord College of Transcendental Knowledge, so they both had to prepare lectures and grade papers. Aunt Alex would be reading a book in the schoolroom, taking notes, when she would suddenly sniff the air and rush to the kitchen to snatch a pot off the stove.

But this time she had spent twenty minutes stirring the spaghetti sauce, never once taking her eyes from the frying pan. Now she served the spaghetti, piling a mound of pasta on everyone's plate and covering it with sauce.

"Where's Uncle Freddy?" said Eddy, who was eager to ask him something.

"I think he's going through a lot of papers," said Aunt Alex.

But then Uncle Freddy came slowly into the kitchen and sat down.

"Uncle Freddy?" said Eddy at once.

"Here you are, dear," said Aunt Alex, handing Uncle Freddy a plate of spaghetti.

But instead of picking up his fork, he gazed mournfully at his plate.

"Uncle Freddy!" said Eddy again.

"But why *don't* they invite me?" said Eleanor. "Holly has an invitation and so does Tracey. Why not me? I mean, tell me, is something the matter with me? Tell me the truth."

"Listen, Uncle Freddy," said Eddy, louder this time.

Eleanor jumped up. "I mean, *look* at me." She stuck out one foot to show off her new shoe, which was exactly the kind the other girls were wearing. She turned around to display her new shirt, which hung down over her skinny hips with exactly the right droop.

She snatched the glasses off her nose and shook them in Aunt Alex's face. "Designer glasses! I ask you, go ahead, tell me what's wrong."

Eddy was sick of not getting a word in edgewise. He looked at his sister slyly. "You really want to know? Well, okay, I'll tell you. A, you're awful, B, you're boring, C, you're crazy, D, you're dumb, E . . ."

Normally Eleanor wouldn't have cared what Eddy said. She would just have kicked him under the table. But at the moment she was in a weird sort of mood. Shrieking, she plunged out of the kitchen and ran upstairs, her feet thumping heavily all the way to the top. Her bedroom door slammed with a mighty crash.

"Oh, dear," sighed Aunt Alex. She looked solemnly across the table and said, "Really, Eddy," then pushed back her chair and followed Eleanor upstairs.

Uncle Freddy and Eddy were left alone with their plates of spaghetti. The kitchen was peaceful without Eleanor's throbbing misery. Eddy tried again. "Uncle Freddy, did you ever hear of time travel?"

Uncle Freddy looked up and seemed to get hold of himself. "Time travel? Of course." At last he picked up his fork and began twisting it in his spaghetti. "There's one really good way to do it."

"You mean people can really travel in time, Uncle Freddy?"

"Oh, I don't know about really." Uncle Freddy put his fork down again and gazed at the calendar on the wall as if he had forgotten his supper and his overexcited nephew.

"No, no, Uncle Freddy, just tell me! Do you think the past is still back there somewhere, waiting to be rediscovered, if you only knew how to do it?"

Uncle Freddy fumbled with his chair and scraped it backward on the floor. He seemed to be looking at his nephew, but Eddy felt transparent, as though his uncle were looking right through him at something far away beyond the front porch of the house and Walden Street and the Mill Brook and Lexington Road.

"Time," Uncle Freddy murmured, "is but the stream I go a-fishing in."

Eddy stared at him. "But Uncle Freddy—"

Then Uncle Freddy came back to himself and laughed. "It's just something Henry said." He pulled his chair in again and wrapped pasta around his fork. This time he put it in his mouth. Strands of spaghetti straggled down his chin.

Eddy was disappointed. "Oh, right," he said. "Henry again." Eddy sighed. He had been listening all his life to the things Henry Thoreau had said, famous things like:

Simplify, simplify, simplify!

or

Old clothes will serve a hero!

or

In wildness is the preservation of the world!

Sometimes Eddy wished Henry had been a dentist and had never written anything at all.

"You can do it too, Eddy," said Uncle Freddy, spearing another forkful. "You can fish in the stream of time. You can go back three thousand years whenever you like."

"Oh, I get it," said Eddy wearily. "You mean I can travel in a book. I can read an old book. Oh, sure."

"That's right," said Uncle Freddy. "That's how you can travel in time, Eddy. You can dangle your hook in a book. You can fish in the ocean of time." He threw up his arm as if flinging out a line. "Fish in the sky!"

His fork clattered to the floor just as Aunt Alex came back into the kitchen with a tearstained Eleanor.

Aunt Alex gave Eddy a look.

There was no way of getting out of it. "I'm sorry, Eleanor," Eddy said gracefully, and then he turned back to his uncle. "But Uncle Freddy, hasn't anybody ever gone back in time? Not just in a book. I mean really? In person?"

Eleanor had recovered from her tantrum, but she was still his bossy sister. "Don't be stupid, Eddy. Time travel just happens in stories."

"Like *The Time Machine*, by H. G. Wells," said Aunt Alex, sitting down and smiling around the table. "Have you ever read *The Time Machine*, Eddy?"

"No," said Eddy, taking a sudden interest. "A time machine! Did it work? Did it really work?"

"Well, in the story it did. But when the inventor went into the future, he got stuck there because his time machine was stolen. And then when he got it back, he tried going millions of years still further into the future, but that was terrible too, because there was nothing left on earth but giant crabs."

"Giant crabs!"

Eleanor spoke up dreamily, leaning her elbows on the table. "Suppose you just wanted something so badly, could you make it happen?" She looked wistfully at her plate. "I mean suppose it just *had* to happen? Your wish could sort of *force* it to happen." Eleanor speared the air with her fork, as if forcing a wish to come true.

"What does that have to do with time travel?" said Eddy scornfully. "That's the dumbest thing I ever heard."

Aunt Alex changed the subject quickly. "Seconds, anybody? Thirds? After the spaghetti there's ice cream."

Eddy grinned at her. "You mean the ice cream won't exist until we eat our spaghetti?"

Aunt Alex laughed. The telephone rang. Eleanor

threw down her spoon, snatched the phone off the wall, and said, "Hello?"

But it wasn't Amanda Upshaw inviting her to the party. Ruefully, Eleanor said, "Just a minute," and handed the phone to Uncle Freddy.

He murmured, "Hello?" and then, "Excuse me a moment. I'll just go to the other telephone."

Surprised, they watched him vanish into the hall.

Eddy ate two helpings of ice cream, and then, while Eleanor went upstairs to spread out a piece of green silk on her bed—she was making a dress for the party—he went back to the triangular corner under the front hall stairs to gloat over the gift from India.

Uncle Freddy's time travel was just something in a book. Eddy's was real. He had *relived* two minutes of his actual life.

The new bike that had traveled halfway around the world in a wooden crate from India was a Time Bike after all.

What should he do with it? Which should he explore, the past or the future? The whole history of the world was his to go a-fishing in, just the way Uncle Freddy said.

But not just in books.

"Fred, dear," said Aunt Alex, "that phone call. Is something the matter?"

"No, no, my dear. Nothing's the matter. Nothing at all."

Aunt Alex looked at him doubtfully, but she said nothing more.

8

BARGING INTO NEXT WEEK

URING THE NIGHT Eddy had a brilliant idea. In the morning he jumped out of bed and pulled on his clothes, thinking it over.

It was exam week, the last week of school. That meant he had to study and study and take exam after exam. At last at the end of the week he would graduate from eighth grade, and Mr. Orth would hand him a diploma and he'd be ready for high school next fall.

What if he got the Time Bike to take him a week into the future? What if he just skipped right over this whole gruesome week to the last day of school? All the studying and exam taking would be over. Summer vacation would begin, and he'd get a job and make enough money to buy a secondhand computer like Oliver Winslow's.

Eddy brushed his teeth, scrubbing fast, working out a plan. Of course he would have to be careful. The bike was on a hair trigger, like a gun that fires when you just barely look at it. Last night he had only jostled the bike, and it had come to life with a bang and swooped him two minutes into the past.

And of course, above all, whatever he did, he mustn't get stuck in some other time like that poor guy in *The Time Machine*.

Eddy galloped downstairs and poked his head into the schoolroom, where Aunt Alex's typewriter was rattling away. "Good morning, Aunt Alex," he said cheerfully.

Aunt Alex banged out another sentence. "Oh, Eddy, your orange juice is on the table, and then there's an English muffin."

"You mean the English muffin won't exist until—"

"Oh, yes, it will." Aunt Alex whipped the paper out of the typewriter and stood up. "This is exam week, isn't it, Eddy?"

"It certainly is. Ab-so-lute-ly! How jolly!"

"Well, good luck, Eddy, dear. I know you'll work hard." Aunt Alex smiled at him and went upstairs.

Eddy was in too much of a hurry to be careful with breakfast. He gulped down the orange juice, toasted the two halves of the English muffin, slathered one half with butter, ate it, shoved the other in his pocket, and charged out into the hall.

Upstairs Eleanor was shouting, "Who took the ironing board? Oh, here it is." And then there were noises of dragging and bumping as she hauled it into her room, set it up on its collapsible legs, and dropped it on her foot. A whimper of pain drifted down the stairs.

He was alone in the front hall. Eddy went to the triangular corner next to the coat closet, lifted the curtain, and pulled it aside to let light fall on his miraculous bicycle. Then very carefully he put his leg over and sat down, lowering his weight slowly, not wanting to squeeze the springs too suddenly or joggle the handlebars.

Leaning forward, he looked at the Time Clock. At once he understood the little plus-and-minus tab on the side. Plus meant the future, minus meant the past. It made perfect sense.

Yesterday the clock had been set for the past, and it had carried him two minutes back in that direction. Delicately Eddy pushed the tab the other way. Now the bike would take him into the future. Then he studied the dial that said:

DAYS

with its 365 spidery marks. With the utmost care he twisted the setscrew until the needle quivered at line number seven. That should take him a week into the future. And then, holding his breath, he pushed down gently on the right pedal.

But the bike was obstinate. It bucked a little, then made a whining noise like grinding gears. The front wheel seemed to be butting against a stone wall, and yet it was still trying to roll forward. There was a smell of burning rubber. The mirror on the handlebars blazed with fire.

Eddy gritted his teeth and hung on, jouncing up and down on the narrow seat, his arms and legs shivering and shaking as if his bones were coming loose. At last, with a smashing roar like the fall of a dynamited building, the bike leaped forward, bumping up and rocking down, as if jolting over stony ground.

Suddenly it jerked to a stop. Eddy pitched over the handlebars and hit his head against the slanting wall under the stairs.

For a moment he lay still, collecting his wits. Then he struggled to his feet, parted the curtain, and stepped out into the front hall.

Everything looked just the same. Had a week really gone by?

The same kind of morning light was glancing

through the oval glass of the front door. Eddy could feel a lump in his pants pocket. It was the English muffin. He pulled it out and looked at it in surprise. It was stiff and stale.

Turning, he watched Eleanor charge past him without a word, heading for the front door, and he heard Aunt Alex call after her, "Wait, dear, you forgot your backpack."

And then, as Eleanor pulled open the door and ran out on the front porch, she shouted back at Aunt Alex something that filled Eddy's heart with joy. "Oh, Aunt Alex, I don't need a backpack. It's the last day of school."

The last day of school! It was next week! He had missed a whole week of hard studying and test taking. It was all over, and he had come out on the other side.

"Ralph?"

It was Madeline Prawn again. Mr. Preek sighed. He was getting a little tired of her daily phone calls. "Now, Madeline, we must be patient. My research continues to look promising. Until now I have found no record of a legal transfer of the property. So far, so good. We can but hope."

"I shall pray," breathed Miss Prawn.

9

EDDY FLUNKS OUT

WAS HE TOO LATE FOR the bus? Eddy looked at his watch. No, he had plenty of time. Briskly he strode to the door, but then Uncle Freddy popped out of the parlor and said gravely, "Eddy, I've had a letter from your school."

"Sorry, Uncle Freddy," said Eddy, grinning at him. "Not now. I'll be late for the bus."

"Well, when you get home this afternoon I need to talk to you."

"Certainly, sir," said Eddy, saluting. "Ab-so-lute-ly, sir. At your service, sir."

Sauntering to the bus stop at the corner of Everett Street, he felt a little ashamed of himself. This time

Uncle Freddy had not smiled at his comic nephew. And he had seemed different somehow, sadder and older. But why? With the magical help of the Time Bike, Eddy had skipped only a week. Uncle Freddy couldn't have become a lot older in a single week.

Nor could he ever be sad, not Uncle Freddy. Even in the bad old days long ago when he had been a little bit crazy, he had never seemed unhappy. Even though people had whispered about him and called him "poor Fred," even in those unhappy days he had been a jolly uncle, a sort of harmless screwball whom everyone loved.

Then, of course, the diamond in the window in the attic had made everything right again, and Uncle Freddy's wits had come back, and now he was a really famous professor. So he was okay now, wasn't he? Wasn't everything better now?

Eddy perked up as he got off the bus, ready to enjoy the last day of the school year.

But somehow it wasn't what he expected. In the hall the other kids looked at him strangely. In science class Frannie Pagett leaned across the aisle and said, "Serves you right, you jerk."

Eddy's old friend Oliver Winslow sat behind him. He punched Eddy in the back and whispered, "God, I'm sorry, Eddy."

Eddy felt a sinking in the pit of his stomach. "Sorry? Sorry about what?"

"Flunking out. You know, you flunked out."

Flunked out! Eddy gasped. How could it have happened? The bike must have betrayed him. The missed week hadn't turned out the way it should.

The bike should have known that he would have studied enough to pass his exams. The real Eddy would never have flunked out, not if he had really lived through every miserable day of the whole entire week.

"Too bad, fella," whispered Oliver.

Oliver's whispers were like hoarse roars. At the front of the room Mrs. Plumwell, the science teacher, looked at him mournfully and began her lecture. "Now, class, I know it's the last day of school, but I hate to end the year without finishing our discussion of something truly *wonderful*"—she coughed nervously—"Newton's laws of motion, the last of which is . . ." She turned her back and wrote on the board—

TO EVERY ACTION THERE IS AN EQUAL
AND OPPOSITE REACTION.

Behind her back the whispering and the shuffling of feet grew louder. Mrs. Plumwell turned around and said patiently, "Now, honestly, class, may I humbly request the favor of your attention for just a few more minutes?"

But it was the last day of school. Kids sprawled in their chairs and grinned at each other and passed around their yearbooks, signing their names beside their pictures and scribbling funny remarks in the margins.

Jackie Brownwell's yearbook was passing down the row, stopping at every desk because Jackie wanted everybody to sign it. When her book reached Eddy, he turned the pages to find his own name.

It wasn't there. A blank piece of paper had been pasted over the space between Marilyn Grossman and Perry Hillside. There was nothing to sign.

Oliver Winslow leaned forward again with his yearbook and showed Eddy his own big grinning face.

"You passed, right?" said Eddy in a hollow whisper.

"Nagmanimous," whispered Oliver loudly. "They were truly nagmanimous."

It wasn't fair. Eddy stared at the words on the blackboard. Oliver Winslow was the worst student in the eighth grade. He wasn't stupid, but he never did any homework. He had been left back two or three times, so he was a lot older than the rest of the class. He even had a driver's license. Last year he had owned a car called the Green Horror, but unfortunately he had totaled it against the side of his father's garage, and now the Green Horror sat in his backyard, a useless wreck. Mr.

Winslow's garage was still in ruins.

So if anybody should have flunked out, it was Oliver Winslow.

Then Eddy forgot about Oliver. Mrs. Plumwell was still trying to talk about Newton's third law. "Action and reaction," she said loudly, but nobody was listening.

Nobody, that is, except Edward Hall. Eddy was listening with all his might.

10

ACTION AND REACTION

*A*CTION AND REACTION. Eddy figured out what had happened. You couldn't get anything out if you didn't put anything in, because everything was in balance.

If you hit a ball with a bat, *wham*, it sailed into the outfield, and the bat shivered like a gong. If you put heat under a pan, the water boiled. If you jumped on the bed, you sailed into the air and the bedsprings went *boing*.

It was horribly simple and clear. Eddy had put no energy into exam week, so he had gotten nothing out. If he wanted to go to high school in the fall, he would have to take makeup courses all summer. So he wouldn't have time for a job. It was sickening.

And of course Eddy's talk with Uncle Freddy was terrible. Uncle Freddy wasn't angry. He was perfectly sober and calm.

Eddy was ashamed, but he was also puzzled. "Listen, Uncle Freddy, didn't you *see* me studying last week?"

"No," said Uncle Freddy shortly, turning back to his book, "I did not."

Eddy couldn't understand it. What had they all been doing last week? If he, Eddy, had lost an entire week of his life, did that mean that everybody else had lost it too? The whole human race? Had the whole entire earth jumped forward a week in its orbit around the sun, all those sextillions of tons of dirt and water and rock?

He went to the kitchen and confronted Aunt Alex, who was beating something with the electric mixer and reading a book at the same time.

The mixer made a lot of noise. "Aunt Alex," shouted Eddy, "what were you doing last week?"

Aunt Alex looked up at him vaguely and turned off the mixer. "What was I doing? I was reading this book. I was reading Henry Thoreau's *Walden*."

Eddy was astonished. "But, Aunt Alex, you've read it fifty times before."

Aunt Alex smiled and scooped her batter into a cake tin.

"Well, what about Eleanor? What was she doing last

53

week?" In Eddy's own ears it sounded like a foolish question. Lamely he added, "I've sort of forgotten what we all did last week."

Aunt Alex gazed into space and licked the spatula. "Oh, Eddy, you know Eleanor. She was waiting for a phone call and staring at the mailbox and working on her party dress."

Suddenly Aunt Alex remembered her hot stove. She snatched up the cake tin and popped it into the oven. "Now, if you'll excuse me, Eddy, our class is about to begin."

The front door banged. There was a bustle in the hall. The students were arriving. Eddy had met them before. They were old friends.

"Hi, there, Eddy," said Arthur Hathaway, clapping him on the back.

"Hello there, Eddy," said Barbara Greenberg, smiling at him.

"Well, if it isn't Edward P. Hall," said Jonathan Jones, giving him a friendly poke.

As they walked into the schoolroom, most of them touched the white plaster shoulder of Henry Thoreau as if it were holy, or maybe just for luck.

Had they missed Eddy last week? Apparently not. It was very mysterious.

In the schoolroom there was a pandemonium of

voices, while they greeted each other and sat down and tumbled open their notebooks. Then they quieted down. Through the velvet curtain Eddy could hear Uncle Freddy beginning to talk.

Sleepily he sat down on the bottom step of the staircase, half listening. A wisp of smoke floated past his nose, and he sniffed. Outdoors the little rooster crowed loudly. Suddenly the schoolroom curtain parted and Aunt Alex burst out and rushed past Eddy into the kitchen. "My cake," she cried. "I forgot my cake."

But it was all right. It was only a little burnt.

II

OLIVER FINDS OUT

THE MAKEUP CLASSES had begun for the kids who had flunked eighth grade.

In the Sanborn School, Eddy went back to his old homeroom to struggle with math and grammar and science and Latin. He couldn't believe he had flunked everything, but he had.

Classes took all morning, and homework all afternoon. There was no time left for a summer job.

Eddy had hoped to work as a clerk in Vanderhoof's Hardware Store and make enough money for the computer he wanted so badly. After all, the whole family needed a computer, whether they knew it or not.

The trouble was, Aunt Alex and Uncle Freddy didn't

have a clue. They bent over their desks writing by hand, or they used the noisy old typewriter in the schoolroom. Sometimes Eddy heard it *rat-a-tat-tatt*ing in the middle of the night.

One night there was another noise, a tumble and thump on the ceiling over Eddy's bed. Someone was upstairs in the attic, bumbling around.

Eddy got out of bed and looked out into the hall. Uncle Freddy was coming down the attic stairs, his shoulders slumped, his face tired and discouraged.

"What were you doing up there in the attic, Uncle Freddy?" said Eddy.

"Oh, I'm sorry, Eddy. Did I wake you up? I was just looking for something."

But whatever Uncle Freddy had been looking for, he hadn't found it, because his hands were empty.

Eddy went back to bed, but he still couldn't sleep. He kept thinking about his big mistake with the Time Bike. If only he hadn't tried to skip the week of exams!

After the first day back at school and the first afternoon of homework, he comforted himself by spending the evening at Oliver Winslow's house watching cop shows on television.

Oliver's mother complained when she brought in a plate of snacks. "Look at that! Another exploding car."

"It's all right, Mrs. Winslow," Eddy said innocently. "Justice will triumph in the end."

When she left the room, still muttering, Eddy turned down the volume. "Oliver," he said, "if you had a time machine, what would you do with it?"

"A time machine?" Oliver didn't hesitate. "I'd go back to last year."

"Only last year? What for?"

"My car was still okay last year," said Oliver, grinning at Eddy.

"The Green Horror? Oh, right."

"I'd go back and get it. Then it wouldn't be just a pile of junk in the backyard. It would still be working."

Eddy laughed. Even when it was working, the Green Horror had been a rattletrap. It was an old Chevy Impala held together with wire and chewing gum. But last year Oliver had driven it all the way to Washington, D.C., in support of the Pilgrimage of Peace, that long parade of kids walking to Washington, following Eddy's little cousin Georgie, with her fragile old flag.

In the gloom of the TV room in the Winslows' house, with his face a sickly green in the light of the television screen and a talk show giggling and chattering in the background, Eddy told Oliver about the Time Bike.

He had to tell somebody, and Oliver was his best friend.

12

BACK TO YESTERDAY

*E*LEANOR WAS STILL HOPING against hope for an invitation. Amanda Upshaw's party was only ten days away. All the really important kids in the tenth grade had been invited already. Girls like Holly and Sandy and Linda, boys like Peter and Charley and Scott.

Michelle hadn't been invited yet, Eleanor knew that, but no wonder. Was Eleanor as unpopular as Michelle Dove? If so, she couldn't stand it.

The last days of June were clear and cool. But Eleanor's longing hung over the house like a cloud.

Uncle Freddy too was lost in thought. He hardly seemed to notice the lovely days and starlit nights.

"Wow," said Eddy to Aunt Alex, "being a selectman

must be an awful pain. Is that why Uncle Freddy is so different? I mean, these days he just seems so different."

Aunt Alex said nothing for a minute, and then she murmured, "I guess he has a lot on his mind."

"Oh, is that it?"

Then Eddy forgot about Uncle Freddy's strangeness. He forgot about his sister's problem. He had his own excitement. He had decided what to do next with the Time Bike. He would try something really simple, just as an experiment.

He would go back to yesterday.

Of course that was only the beginning. Sooner or later Eddy wanted to range freely over all past history. He would watch great battles and meet famous people like Julius Caesar and William Shakespeare and Abraham Lincoln.

On his flimsy little bike he'd be a swashbuckling explorer of time. As famous as the astronauts who went to the moon.

And instead of their tired old motto, "One small step for man, one giant leap for mankind," there'd be a fabulous new slogan: "One small step for a boy, one giant leap into history for the entire human race!"

Only of course it wasn't really a step, it was a spinning whirl, a wild and glorious ride on Eddy's wonderful, magical bicycle.

From now on he would take things slow. He'd just go back to yesterday.

But not right away. He'd have to wait through a whole week of makeup classes, because there was no point in reliving a day of hard work at school. On Saturday he'd be sure to have a lot of fun, and then on Sunday he'd use the Time Bike to live the fun over again.

There was no problem about how to have fun. Every Saturday afternoon in the summertime a bunch of Eddy's friends played baseball at the Emerson Park Playground, with Mr. Orth as referee.

When Saturday came, it was fun, all right, although right fielder Eddy lost the game for his side when a ground ball bounced right past him. Well, that was okay. It would give him a chance to find out if he could change the past.

This time he'd know which way the ball was going to bounce. He'd pick it up and hurl it to home base, and the runner would be out.

Sunday was a rainy day. The curtained corner under the stairs was even darker than usual.

Eddy twisted the neck of the gooseneck lamp on Aunt Alex's desk so that it shone on the bicycle when he pulled back the curtain. Then he leaned over the handlebars of the Time Bike and examined the clock with great care.

He mustn't make a mistake. Very gently he moved the hand of the dial that numbered days, until it rested on the first narrow line. Then he lowered the tab on the side of the clock to the minus sign at the bottom of the slot, to send the bike into the past instead of the future.

There, was he ready?

Eddy sat down on the high seat and clutched the handlebar grips with both hands. The bicycle was trembling as if it were ready to go. The headlight made a wobbling blob of light like a jewel on the wall of the coat closet. The telephone was ringing in the front hall, and the bicycle wheels made a whirring noise as they began to turn, and there was a softer sound, too—what was that?—like the murmur of waves rolling up on a sandy beach.

But the bike did not take him to the seashore—it took him to the Emerson Park Playground in the very middle of the town of Concord, Massachusetts, and to the Saturday-afternoon baseball game, just the way he wanted it to.

But at the last minute he caught a glimpse of something in the little round mirror on the handlebars, a pair of staring eyes. They were not Eddy's. Whose were they?

13

HISTORY REPEATS ITSELF

WHACK! OLIVER WINSLOW was at bat. Oliver could hit like anything, but this time it was only a foul tip. The girl at third base picked it up and tossed it to the big kid who was pitching for the other side.

Oliver thudded his bat on home plate and hoisted it again, ready for the next pitch, but of course it was no use, because he was about to hit a pop fly. Eddy had seen it before. This was *yesterday's* ball game.

The only difference was that this time he, Eddy, *the Eddy from tomorrow,* wasn't taking part in it—he was sitting on the Time Bike under the bleachers watching it happen, while the Eddy from yesterday sat right there

63

on the front bench between Arlo and Lawrence only a few feet away.

Would anybody notice that there were two Eddys at the ball game? Eddy edged his bike farther back in the shadows. It was really weird to see his own skinny back and hear his own voice yell, "Go for it, Oliver!" But of course Oliver's pop fly sailed high into the air and came down with a plop in the glove of the right fielder.

Oliver's mother was there again, watching the game. She clapped loyally as Oliver dropped his bat and loped to his position at second base, and the other Eddy jumped up from the bench and headed for his place in the outfield.

The real Eddy watched sadly from the forest of timbers under the bleachers as history repeated itself. There was nothing he could do to change what was about to happen. He knew which way the grounder was going to bounce, but he couldn't run out there and tell the other Eddy. That wouldn't do any good. Everybody would yell and scream and the game would come to a crashing halt.

There was a shout from Mr. Orth, "Get it, Eddy, get it." And everybody else was yelling too, "Come on, Eddy, get it." And then of course the excited shouts became disappointed groans.

He couldn't look. Eddy turned his head away, not

wanting to see the batter on the other team gallop around the bases for the winning run. At once he saw Hunky Poole.

Hunky was watching the game furtively from the sidewalk on the other side of the chain-link fence. Like Eddy, he was sitting on a bicycle with his feet on the ground. And the bike was Eddy's. It was his own birthday bike, his brand-new Timuri, shiny and red, with its rock shocks and twenty-one combinations of gears. It was the bike Aunt Alex and Uncle Freddy had paid so much money for, the beautiful bike that had been Eddy's pride and joy.

That sleazeball Hunky had crept up on the front porch in the dark of night and grabbed it. Hunky Poole had stolen Eddy's bike!

Angrily, Eddy told himself there was nothing he could do about it now. He had discovered to his sorrow that he couldn't interfere with things that had already happened—he couldn't change anything about yesterday. But when he got back to tomorrow, he'd get his bike back. He'd go after Hunky Poole.

The light was dim and shadowy under the bleachers. Eddy had to crouch low over the clockwork on the handlebars of the Time Bike to change the minus switch to plus and move the delicate needle forward.

Then, while everybody milled around and the kids

on the winning team grinned and punched each other and Oliver slapped yesterday's Eddy on the back and Mrs. Winslow groped in her pocketbook and pulled out a couple of candy bars, Eddy pushed down on the pedal of his bike.

But just as he felt it wobble forward, he saw Hunky Poole looking straight at him. Hunky's eyes were widening in surprise—they were the eyes Eddy had seen in the little round mirror on the handlebars. They were staring from one Eddy to the other. They were staring at the Time Bike.

Then Hunky Poole and Oliver Winslow and Oliver's mother and the Eddy of yesterday dimmed and disappeared, along with the sunshine, and almost at once Eddy found himself back in the rainy Sunday of today.

He was back in the shadowy corner under the front hall stairs, and the telephone was still ringing.

He heard Eleanor snatch it up and say, "Hello!" But of course the call was for somebody else, Uncle Freddy this time, because nobody was inviting poor old Eleanor to any dumb old party.

Eddy got off the bike and rolled it out from under the stairs. As Uncle Freddy came out of the schoolroom to answer the phone, Eddy walked the bike to the back door.

Outside on the porch, while the rain fell on the

chicken yard and the chickens lurked in their little house and the laundry drooped damply on the line, Eddy looked at the Time Bike, examining it all over, from the balloon tires to the upright handlebars, from the ruby reflector in back to the headlight in front.

The headlight shone on the laundry, making a glimmering spot on a wet shirt of Uncle Freddy's. The battery had not run down after all. Probably it would never run down. The headlight would shine forever. It would still be shining when the sun cooled down and the earth stopped turning and there was nothing left but giant crabs.

And there on the water-soaked porch, perched on the saddle of the Time Bike with his head lowered and his arms folded on his chest and a mist of raindrops blowing across his face, Eddy thought hard about the events of his backward trip into yesterday.

Eddy was good at thinking, whenever he could slow down the skip and frolic of his brain. The question he asked himself was simple. Could he or couldn't he alter what had happened in the past? This morning it had been impossible, because the whole thing had been a repeat of something he had taken part in himself, only yesterday.

But suppose he went back to a time before he had been born? In the really distant past he would be a perfect stranger. And then perhaps he could change things a little, jerk them sideways, nudge them into different shapes. Maybe he could correct some of the things that had gone so horribly wrong in the past, terrible things that had messed up everything that had happened later on. Why not? He could save the human race from its own mistakes. He himself, Edward P. Hall, citizen of Concord at the beginning of the third millennium in the great onward progress of the centuries, could be a pathfinder, a benefactor, a time-traveling hero.

Smiling, Eddy leaned the Time Bike against the wall of the house between a pair of flapping sheets. Then, puffed up with a sense of his own importance, he went back inside and slammed the screen door. He was just in time to see Uncle Freddy put down the phone and bow his head.

For a moment Eddy forgot his own sensational destiny. He looked at his uncle with concern, and said, "Are you all right, Uncle Freddy?"

At once Uncle Freddy squared his shoulders and smiled at him. "Of course I am, Eddy."

But when he turned away and started up the stairs, his shoulders sagged and his smile was gone.

14

STOLEN AGAIN

*T*HE FACT THAT EDDY COULD change the past and make things different in the present was proved right away. Hunky Poole came again in the night and stole the Time Bike.

Aunt Alex discovered it next morning. "Eddy, dear," she called up the stairs, "did you bring in your bike? I saw it on the back porch last night when I went out to feed the chickens, but it's not there now, and I don't see it anywhere."

Eddy sprang out of bed and lunged downstairs and charged out onto the laundry porch. The morning sun slanted across the chicken yard, where the boastful little rooster was crowing, "*ARK-ARK-AROOOOOO,*" and the laundry still hung on the line.

But the Time Bike was gone.

"Hunky Poole!" shouted Eddy, slamming into the house again, banging the screen door. "Hunky Poole stole it. He stole the other bike too. I know he did, I saw it. Hunky Poole's got both my bikes."

Eleanor couldn't believe it. "Two bikes? You've lost two bikes? How could one stupid kid lose two whole bikes?"

Eddy felt terrible. Last night he should have brought the bike inside, because if Hunky Poole could steal one bike from the front porch, he could steal the other from the back.

One stupid kid! He was stupid, all right!

But then Eddy looked so miserable, his sister relented and said kindly, "Why don't you call the police?"

"Not now," said Aunt Alex. "I'm sorry, Eddy, dear, but you'll be late for school."

"After school," said Uncle Fred, looking at him gravely. "You can report it to the police right after school."

The police station was only a quarter of a mile away from the house at No. 40 Walden Street, just around the curve of the road on the way to Route 2.

When Eddy got off the bus that afternoon, he ran home, dumped his books on the front porch, and set off to report to the police the theft of two bicycles by Hunky Poole.

He was steaming with anger and frustration. It had been bad enough to lose his glorious birthday bike, but losing the Time Bike was much worse—in fact it was absolutely horrible.

Hunky didn't know what the bike could do, he didn't know how to be careful. The thought of Hunky blundering around in time was unthinkable. But it could happen. It might really be happening right now.

The officer at the desk in the police station listened to Eddy's complaint, and wrote down descriptions of the missing bicycles. "You say you saw this boy Hunky with one of the bikes? What's his real name?"

"Harold," said Eddy angrily. "Harold Poole."

"Did you see him with the other bike? How do you know he took it?"

"I just know."

The officer sighed. "Well, all right. We'll go to this kid's house and speak to him."

Sitting beside the police officer in the cruiser, Eddy couldn't stop thinking of the awful catastrophe that Hunky might be creating right now, knocking around in centuries past or centuries to come, messing everything

71

up. The policeman didn't know how hugely important it was to get the bike back.

Hunky lived in a neat Cape Cod house on Lexington Road. His mother answered the bell by opening the door only an inch and staring warily at them through the crack.

"Is your son at home?" said the officer. He looked at his notes. "I'd like to talk to Harold."

"You got a warrant?" said Mrs. Poole quickly, giving Eddy a piercing glance.

"Ma'am, we don't need a warrant to talk to the boy. Is he here?"

Mrs. Poole stared at the officer for a moment without speaking, and then she said, "Just a minute." She ducked back and slammed the door.

"Why don't you go inside and look?" said Eddy angrily. "You're giving him time to hide them. He could hide a rhinoceros in there while we're stuck here outside."

"Relax, kid," said the officer, sighing deeply. The shiny buttons on his navy-blue chest rose and fell.

It was a long wait. "You see?" muttered Eddy, but then the door opened. Mrs. Poole thrust Hunky outside, then slammed the door again.

Hunky was a short thick boy with bold eyes that stared straight at you. "What do you want?" he said.

"You selling tickets to the policeman's ball?" He looked at Eddy and grinned. "Well, if it isn't Effie Hall. What the heck you doing here, Effie?" Then Hunky used a four-letter word. It made the police officer mad.

"Listen here, young man," said the officer, "there's no need for that kind of language. This is a serious matter. My young friend thinks you have stolen his bicycles."

"Me? Steal Effie Hall's dumb old bikes? What would I do that for?"

"I saw you at the baseball game with my new bike," cried Eddy.

"The heck you did. I didn't have no bike at baseball."

"I was under the bleachers. I saw it. My bike!"

Hunky laughed. "That's crap. I haven't got your stinking bike."

Mrs. Poole had been listening. She threw up a window and said, "You can't search the premises without you got a search warrant."

The police officer looked tired. He glowered at Hunky. "You swear that you did not take any property belonging to Edward Hall? Remember, young man, lying to a police officer is a misdemeanor."

Hunky grinned. "I swear I didn't take any crappy old bike from Effie Hall."

The policeman lost patience. "Repeat after me. 'I

swear I did not take any property belonging to Edward Hall.'"

Hunky repeated it in a silly voice.

There was nothing more to be done. Mrs. Poole banged down the window. Hunky withdrew into the house and slammed the door.

Eddy walked back to the car with the officer, fuming. "But he's got them in there—you know he does. Can't we come back with a search warrant?"

The officer looked at him sadly. "If we came back with a warrant, do you think we'd find any bikes in that house?"

"Well, maybe not."

At home Eddy stumped up the porch steps, feeling outraged.

Aunt Alex was there, opening the door, looking at him with bright sympathy. "No bike?"

Eddy shook his head angrily. "No bike."

"Oh, Eddy, dear, I'm sorry."

15

THE BIKE COMES BACK

*E*DDY FELT MORE MISERABLE than he had ever felt before in all his life. He couldn't decide what to do. He couldn't get out of his head the vision of Hunky Poole cluttering up the past and destroying the future. Messing up the whole wide world!

Eddy's sister was careful not to taunt him. Eleanor could have said, "Serves you right," but she didn't. His misery was too plain. She left him alone. She sat at the sewing machine in her bedroom, working on her dress.

The sewing machine droned and paused and droned again. Eleanor liked to sew. It was the one thing that calmed the tumult in her heart. Swiftly she ran the needle down a side seam. The dress would be perfect for Amanda Upshaw's party.

But the party was only a few days away, and Eleanor had almost given up hope of finding an invitation in the mailbox, or of hearing Amanda's voice on the phone—"Oh, Eleanor, I'm just so incredibly sorry to be late, but can you come to my party?"

Briskly, Eleanor lifted the needle of the sewing machine, whisked the dress around, and began stitching another seam. She had forgotten about Eddy.

But she was standing right beside him when the Time Bike came back.

It was after supper on one of the longest days of the year. Only very slowly did the warm light of sunset give way to dusk, and then to a darkening of the summer sky.

Eddy happened to be standing on the top step of the porch, staring gloomily in the direction of Hunky Poole's house, when Eleanor came up behind him and grabbed his arm and said, "Look, Eddy, what's that?"

Then Eddy saw it too, the light moving along Lexington Road, there beyond the Mill Brook field. It was a silvery gleam moving rapidly from right to left, a soft trembling ray shining on the hedges beside the road as it ran smoothly in the direction of Monument Square. They watched as it turned left on Heywood Street and came closer and closer and made another left turn onto Walden.

"It's my bike," whispered Eddy.

"The new one? You mean Hunky's bringing it back?"

"No," murmured Eddy. "Nobody's bringing it back. It's coming back by itself."

He held his breath as the Time Bike slowed down and came to a stop in front of their own gate, like a faithful dog. Eddy ran to open the gate, and at once the bike moved forward until the front wheel gently nudged his knees.

It likes me, thought Eddy. *It knows it's my bike.*

Tenderly he grasped the handlebars and lifted the bike up the porch steps, walked it back into the house, and set it down in its own corner under the stairs. For a minute he stroked the front fender, smiling to himself, and then he went to tell Uncle Freddy and Aunt Alex.

"My bike's back," he said, putting his head through the schoolroom curtain.

But Eleanor had already told them the good news.

"Oh, I'm so glad," said Aunt Alex, beaming at Eddy.

"This time we'd better lock all the doors," said Uncle Freddy solemnly, getting to his feet.

It wasn't easy. The locks on the front and back doors were rusty. The doors hadn't been locked in thirty years.

Uncle Freddy went down to the basement for a can of 3 IN 1 oil and squirted it into the keyholes to loosen the tumblers. The oil did the trick. "There," he said, "that will take care of it."

Eddy went to bed feeling secure about his bike.

But he was wrong. Oh, it was true that the bike was safe from any greedy thief like Hunky Poole who might try to break into the house from outside. But as Eddy would find out later, much later, it was not safe from a robber within.

Next morning when he came down to breakfast, he saw his sister's feet below the curtain under the stairs.

"Hey," said Eddy angrily, "what do you think you're doing?"

Eleanor came out from behind the curtain and gave him a piercing look. "Tell me," she said. "It's not just ordinary, right? It's not just a plain ordinary bike?"

Eddy thought for a minute. Telling Oliver Winslow about the bike was probably a mistake, but it wasn't Eddy's fault that Eleanor had been standing right beside him when the bike found its way home last night, all by itself.

There was no getting out of it. And besides, there was something exciting about telling such a wonderful secret. "Come out on the back porch," he said mysteriously.

And on the back porch Eddy told his sister what the bike could do, what it had done already, and what he hoped it would do for him again. There was no one to overhear the secret. Only the leaves of the trees had ears.

Eleanor listened carefully, then went upstairs to her bedroom and stared thoughtfully out the window. Except for Amanda Upshaw's glorious party, Eddy's bike was front and center in her mind.

The party came first, of course, because being left out was so terrible.

"Oh, Madeline," said Ralph Preek testily, "it's you again."

"Forgive me, Ralph, but I simply had to call. Surely you have more news for me by now?"

Mr. Preek spoke solemnly. "Only this, Madeline. In spite of the fact that the man in question has had plenty of warning, he has not yet produced a legal document. Until he does, you have nothing to fear."

"Oh, heaven be praised."

16

A FAVOR FOR UNCLE FREDDY

ELEANOR KNEW ABOUT the Time Bike, and so did Oliver Winslow and Hunky Poole. But it was Eddy's own personal bike, his own special time-traveling bike. If he was ever going to explore past history, to be a far-ranging voyager in time, he'd better get going.

But next morning Eddy didn't wake up until Aunt Alex's bantam rooster crowed noisily from the chicken yard, *"Come on, ladies, here's a juicy bug."*

The rooster was as good as an alarm clock. Eddy bounced out of bed, eager to get the school day over with. As he ran downstairs, he gave a loving glance at the curtained space under the stairs where his bike was waiting for him.

Where in the past should he go? How far back? A short way or a long way? It was so hard to choose. All those bygone centuries were calling to him, reaching out welcoming arms.

School was as boring as usual. Eddy endured the long morning in a saintly fashion, but he rocketed out of the bus when it brought him home, and raced up the porch steps.

They were all in the kitchen, eating lunch. That is, Aunt Alex was eating lunch. Uncle Freddy was staring gloomily at the sandwich on his plate, and Eleanor was hunched over a piece of paper, writing something in fancy letters. Curlicues spiraled out in all directions.

You are invited
to a party

Eddy was disgusted, but Aunt Alex felt only sympathy. Poor Eleanor, she was still breaking her heart over

Amanda Upshaw's party. Oh, if only the dear girl would forget about the party, if only she didn't have this terrible obsession.

Eddy didn't care about his sister's obsession. He had one of his own. He sat down in his chair with a thump and turned to Uncle Freddy to ask an eager question. "What would you do if you could go back in time, Uncle Freddy?"

His uncle still seemed lost in thought, but when Eddy said, "Hey, Uncle Freddy!" he looked up and apologized. "I'm sorry, Eddy. What did you say?"

"I said, what would you do if you could travel in time?"

Eleanor glanced up and looked at Eddy keenly, then lowered her head and made another curlicue. Then, dissatisfied with her homemade invitation, she ripped it in two and began making a sign for her bedroom door:

PRIVATE! KEEP OUT!
THIS MEANS YOU!

Uncle Freddy stared at Eddy blankly, and then he looked across the table at Aunt Alex. "My dear, what would you do if you could travel in time?"

She laughed. "Well, I think we would both do the same thing."

"What, Aunt Alex?" said Eddy. "What would you do?"

But she got up and began collecting dishes and taking them to the sink. Uncle Freddy abandoned his sandwich and picked up a towel.

"Uncle Freddy!" said Eddy. "Come on, tell me. What *would* you do?"

His uncle took a wet glass from Aunt Alex and swabbed it dry. "Well, what do you think I'd do, Eddy?"

"Oh, oh, I get it. You'd go back to Henry's time. You'd visit Henry Thoreau."

Aunt Alex looked over her shoulder and smiled at Eddy. Uncle Freddy said nothing, but it was clear that Eddy had guessed right.

So then it came to him like a flash, and he grinned as he picked up his tunafish sandwich. Now he knew where to go first. He would do a favor for Uncle Freddy and Aunt Alex. He'd go back into Henry's life and come back and tell them all about it.

The phone rang. Eleanor's pencil stopped in the middle of a heart-shaped curlicue, and she looked up.

Aunt Alex dried her soapy hands and answered it. Then, glancing at Eleanor, she said, "Yes, of course. She's right here."

Eleanor leaped up. The call had come at last! Eagerly she took the phone and breathed a trembling hello.

Her face fell. Aunt Alex went back to the dishpan, pretending not to listen as Eleanor said in a tight voice, "Oh, I'm sorry, Michelle, I can't. No, I'm really sorry, but I can't."

Putting down the phone, she stared wildly at Aunt Alex. "Michelle! She wants me to come over. *Michelle Dove.*"

Eddy snickered. "Michelle Dove? You mean that fat little kid with the thick glasses?"

"What's the matter with Michelle Dove?" asked Uncle Freddy mildly.

Eleanor could feel a sob rising in her throat. "Oh, you know, she's not—she's just not . . ."

She couldn't finish. She snatched up her "KEEP OUT" sign, burst out of the kitchen, and charged up the stairs.

"She's not what?" asked Uncle Freddy, baffled.

"She's not one of the best kids," said Aunt Alex softly.

The doorbell rang in the front hall. The cuckoo

clucked on the wall. The rooster crowed in the back-yard.

"Open the door, will you, Eddy?" cried Aunt Alex, pulling off her apron.

Uncle Freddy plunged across the hall to the school-room with an armful of books.

Eddy went to the front door and threw it open for the students in Aunt Alex and Uncle Freddy's school— Arthur Hathaway and Barbara Greenberg and all the rest.

Everybody greeted everybody, and soon all the students were sitting quietly on the schoolroom chairs, listening to Aunt Alex as she stood at the front of the room and began to talk.

Eddy winked at the plaster bust of Henry Thoreau and strode importantly down the hall. He was feeling generous. He was about to do a favor for Uncle Freddy, who seemed so worried these days, who had too much on his mind.

Just wait, Uncle Freddy. This will cheer you up.

As he pulled aside the curtain to look at the Time Bike, his sister yelled down the stairs, "Eddy, have you got a thumbtack?"

"No, I don't," shouted Eddy, because he had better things to do than look for thumbtacks. His bike was waiting for him.

Its wheels were already humming, the headlight was shining, the clock murmured like waves of the sea, and the little mirror sparkled with sunshine. The bike was impatient to get going.

But as Eddy bent over the clock, he realized with a shock that he didn't know how to set it. What was the right year for Henry?

Quickly he went to the archway that divided the front hall from the schoolroom and peered through the gap in the curtains.

And there it was on the board in white chalk. Aunt Alex was writing exactly what he needed to know:

HENRY DAVID THOREAU, 1817

If Eddy had watched Aunt Alex for only another second, he would have seen her add the date of Henry Thoreau's death, 1862.

But he didn't. He hurried back down the hall, mounted the Time Bike, and adjusted the delicate needle to the year 1817.

At once the obedient bicycle began vaulting into the past.

17

HENRY HIMSELF, IN PERSON

HIS TIME THE JOURNEY took longer. After all, the year 1817 was almost two hundred years back.

It streaked past him, the time between now and then. The images in the little round mirror changed so quickly, they made him dizzy—disappearing houses, shrinking trees, a horse and cart, a burning barn.

Eddy bowed his head and squeezed his eyes shut against the buffeting wind of the years as they collapsed backward. His heart thumped, and he gripped the handlebars tighter and tighter.

He was thrilled, because this was what time travel was all about. He wasn't just tiptoeing into yesterday or limping a timid week into the future. He was rushing into a remote era, speeding back and back to an age before he was born.

Alone of the whole human race, alone among all the billions of people on earth, he would see what the world had been like long ago. And he'd be able to tell Aunt Alex and Uncle Freddy something that Henry Thoreau had actually said, his own living words.

When the bike began to slow down at last, Eddy opened his eyes. He saw the flip-flopping of the last days and nights and then a heaving darkness, followed at once by a glowing sunrise. He blinked uncomfortably as the sun surged up and zigzagged back and forth, then came to rest at the top of the sky.

How long had he been holding his breath? Eddy let it go and looked around, feeling dizzy and sick.

The Time Bike had stopped in the middle of a lilac bush. Rusty blossoms brushed his face. Sharp twigs lashed his cheeks. In front of his eyes a beetle was making its way across a leaf. It occurred to Eddy that the beetle's descendants were probably crawling around at this very moment on the leaves of lilac bushes in his own time, in the third millennium. This ancient beetle must be their great-great-great-great-grandfather.

It seemed unconcerned with the fact that it was only a remote piece of history. It went right on climbing sturdily up the leaf, then paused to think things over.

Eddy stepped down, feeling the life in the bike die away as he put one foot on the ground. Thrusting the branches aside, he blundered out of the bush.

Where was he? He had expected to find himself in the woods near Walden Pond, right next to the small shingled house that Henry had built on the shore.

There was no pond in sight, nor any small house in the woods. But there was a bigger house of rough unpainted boards, turned silvery gray by the sun. Chickens stepped daintily here and there in the yard, pecking at the dirt. They weren't small like Aunt Alex's bantams. They were sturdy-looking fat brown hens.

The door of the house was open. Eddy heard a baby cry indoors.

It was a farm, a real old Concord farm. Back in this early time most of the town had been farms like this, not real estate developments with split-level houses and asphalt driveways and swimming pools. Henry was probably out there in the field, plowing or feeding the pigs.

Boldly, Eddy walked toward the house, moving carefully through a feathery rush of chickens. He was delighted to see a woman sitting on a backless chair in front of the shed. She was milking a cow.

Except on television, Eddy had never seen anyone milk a cow, but there was no question about it, this woman was actually milking a real live cow. It was a thin, bony cow, some old-fashioned kind of farm animal, and while she milked it, the cow lowered its head to munch at tufts of grass.

Eddy moved up behind the woman and stood waiting, not wanting to startle her by speaking up to say hello. She was pulling at the cow's teats, squeezing and releasing, while a stream of thin-looking milk spurted into a bucket and rattled against the side. The only other sound was the light chirping of birds from the other side of the road.

And then once again the baby cried.

At once the woman stood up and pulled the bucket out from under the cow. Then she saw Eddy and stopped short.

He started toward her, grinning with all his teeth. "Good morning, ma'am," he said. "Is Henry at home?"

She stared at him blankly. She was a healthy-looking woman wearing an apron over a long, drab dress. Her hair was tucked into a cap tied under her chin.

"What did you say, boy?"

"I said isn't this where Henry lives?" said Eddy. "Henry Thoreau?"

"Henry Thoreau! There's no Henry here." She started for the house with her bucket of milk, then looked back at him, her eyes glimmering with amusement. "Unless you mean *David* Henry Thoreau?"

"Oh, yes," said Eddy, realizing he had made a mistake.

"Well, just a minute, boy." The woman disappeared into the house, carrying the bucket. Eddy waited. A moment later she came back, holding a baby. "Here he is, boy. This is David Henry Thoreau. He's ten days old."

Eddy gaped at the baby. He didn't know what to say. "Well, he sure is cute," he mumbled at last. But the baby wasn't cute. David Henry's little face was purple, he was whimpering and squirming, and he was ugly as sin.

Eddy backed away. "I'm sorry to disturb you," he said lamely.

David Henry Thoreau's mother looked at him and said dryly, "That's all right, boy." Then she turned away and went back inside the house.

Eddy fled back to his bike and clambered aboard and adjusted the clock to deliver him home again, to return him to his own house and his own time.

But just before he was whisked away from the old Thoreau homestead on Virginia Road in the old town of Concord in the year 1817, Eddy caught a last glimpse of the empty front door and heard one more bellow from the baby inside.

Henry Thoreau was telling the world exactly what he thought, but it was not the sort of remark Eddy had hoped to hear.

18

The Department of Missing Correspondence

*I*T WAS THE DAY OF Amanda Upshaw's party.

Eleanor knew exactly what was happening. Amanda was probably at the country club right now, decorating it with a thousand balloons. The florist was driving up in a van full of gigantic dahlias, some guy in the band was polishing his saxophone and blatting a few loud notes, and the lead singer was running his fingers through his matted hair.

But there was still one last feeble spark of hope. After lunch Eleanor walked firmly up Walden Street to the post office and leaned importantly over the counter.

"I'm expecting a letter," she said, "but it's lost in the mail. So I'd like to speak to someone in the Department of Missing Correspondence."

"Missing Correspondence?" The clerk seemed shocked. "We don't have a Department of Missing Correspondence." And then she recited the famous words about the United States Post Office: "'Neither snow, nor rain, nor heat, nor gloom of night stays these couriers from the swift completion of their appointed rounds.' So you see, there's no missing correspondence. The mail always goes through."

"Oh, I see," said Eleanor, crestfallen. She had been hoping that her invitation from Amanda Upshaw had been lost in the shuffle. Now all hope was gone.

On the way home she ran into one of her classmates. It was horribly embarrassing. "Hello, Eleanor," said Becky Haroutunian sweetly. "Hey, like what are you going to wear to Amanda's party?"

There was an awkward pause. Eleanor could feel herself blushing. "Well, the trouble is, I can't come to the party because I'm going away." She fumbled in her brain for a place she might be going away to. "France. I'm taking a plane to Paris, France."

Becky's eyes widened in a look of spiteful triumph. It was easy to guess the truth. Eleanor Hall had not been invited to Amanda's party. Poor Eleanor!

Eleanor felt terrible. Becky walked away up the street, but that dopey fat girl, Michelle Dove, suddenly appeared from behind Eleanor and fell in step beside her, grinning.

It was a conspiratorial grin. Eleanor knew exactly what it meant: *You and I are the only ones not invited to Amanda's party. We have such a lot in common.*

Eleanor didn't want to have *anything* in common with Michelle Dove. But she couldn't pretend not to see her. She gave her a cool glance, then looked away and said distantly, "Oh, hi, there, Michelle."

"You don't have television, do you?" said Michelle. "Want to come to my house tonight and watch *Gone with the Storm*?"

Gone with the Storm! Eleanor looked at Michelle and gasped. In spite of herself, she was tempted. *Gone with the Storm* was a big hit movie from the nineteen thirties. The star was that fantastically romantic and handsome tragic hero Derek Alabaster.

Everybody knew about Derek Alabaster. He was the most famous movie star in history, and *Gone with the Storm* was the most glorious movie ever made.

"Why, thank you, Michelle," said Eleanor. "Well, yes, I guess I'll come. I mean, okay, sure, of course I will."

19

DEREK ALABASTER

NEXT MORNING ELEANOR came down to breakfast very late, because *Gone with the Storm* had lasted until midnight.

Aunt Alex had called at ten thirty, but Mrs. Dove, shouting above the boom of cannonfire, had explained that the film wasn't finished yet. She hoped Eleanor could stay until the end.

"Oh, well, all right," said Aunt Alex. But then she and Uncle Freddy stayed awake, reading in bed, until they heard Eleanor come in.

"Sshh," said Aunt Alex, when Uncle Freddy began to get up. "Never mind. It's all right."

At breakfast Aunt Alex was pleased to discover that

Amanda Upshaw's party had vanished from Eleanor's mind. All she could talk about was *Gone with the Storm* and the leading man, that great superstar of the nineteen thirties, Derek Alabaster.

"If we had a TV set," said Eddy, "we could see movies like that all the time."

"Not like *Gone with the Storm*," said Eleanor reverently. "And there's never been another actor like Derek Alabaster."

"What about that other old movie star Gary Stewart?" said Eddy. He rolled his eyes. "I thought you were just *crazy* about Gary Stewart."

"Oh, Gary Stewart." Eleanor hesitated, then said stoutly, "Gary Stewart was okay, I guess, but he was nothing like Derek Alabaster."

Aunt Alex was amused. Dear Eleanor! Once again she was bewitched. As always, the poor child wanted too much out of life.

But even Aunt Alex didn't know all the things Eleanor had wanted in the past.

At five years old she had believed in fairies. Again and again she had tried to see them dancing in the moonlight.

At nine she forgot about fairies, because now she believed in angels. Night after night Eleanor gazed into the darkest corner of her bedroom, hoping to see one appear in a haze of gold.

At eleven she forgot about angels and began having crushes on boys.

The first was a boy in her sixth-grade class, Benjamin Parks. Later on it was John Green, one of Uncle Freddy's students, and then just last summer a boy named Robert Toby, who lived right around the corner. Robert was more interested in butterflies than girls, but to Eleanor he had seemed really glamorous because he was the grandson of the President of the United States.

The grandson of the President! To Eleanor, Robert had been surrounded by a haze of gold, just like the angel that had never appeared in the darkness of her bedroom.

And now it was a movie star who had been dead for sixty years.

"Mrs. Dove told me Derek Alabaster died in a car wreck and never made another movie," said Eleanor, her eyes shining with tears.

"As a matter of fact," said Uncle Freddy, coming out from behind his newspaper, "he died right here in Concord."

"In Concord!" Eleanor was flabbergasted. "He did?"

"I read about it in the minutes of the Board of Selectmen. The town of Concord put on a big party for him in nineteen thirty-eight, a huge celebration in Monument Square. Everybody wanted his autograph, and he gave a speech, and then he drove away and smashed his car into a tree."

"How terrible," sighed Eleanor.

Eddy looked up from his bowl of cereal, interested for the first time. "What kind of car was it?"

"Oh, Eddy," said Eleanor, "what difference does that make?"

"It was probably a white Rolls-Royce," said Eddy, pouring milk on his shredded wheat, splashing it over the top of the bowl. "Or a Studebaker Convertible Roadster. Movie stars in the nineteen thirties, they all had big fancy cars."

Eleanor ignored her little brother. "Were you at the party, Uncle Freddy?" she asked wistfully.

"Good heavens, no. I wasn't even born yet. Well, after all, it was over sixty years ago, and look at me, I'm still a young thing." Uncle Freddy was trying bravely to make a joke, but his heart wasn't in it.

Aunt Alex reached across the table and took his hand.

"I'll go to the library," said Eleanor, "and ask about the party for Derek Alabaster. You can find out *anything* in the library."

20

A BETTER PARTY

O F COURSE ELEANOR was right. She found exactly
what she wanted in the Concord Library. Soon
she was sitting in the reading room under the
eyes of the painted portraits on the wall, looking at a
printout of the front page of the *Concord Journal* of
August 16, 1938.

There was a headline—

CONCORD THROWS PARTY
FOR DEREK ALABASTER!

Most of the page was taken up with a black-and-
white photograph of a huge crowd of people, all crushed

together, the men in felt hats, the women in summer dresses. They were staring at somebody in the middle of the picture, but all you could see was the top of his head.

Of course it was Derek Alabaster. Eleanor recognized his boyish cowlick. He was standing on a platform in front of the Civil War Memorial, but a lot of people had climbed up in front of him, and they were holding up their autograph books for him to sign.

They were in the way. The photographer must have been cross.

Eleanor peered at the picture, studying every detail. And then her heart skipped a beat. Behind the crowds, behind the top of Derek's head, there was an automobile, a long, gleaming, elegant car.

It was the Death Car! The car the great star was about to wreck on the highway, the car in which he was going to die. Oh, if only someone had persuaded him to take the train.

Tragic, it was so tragic. Eleanor gulped down a sob.

The reference librarian looked at her. "Are you all right, Eleanor?"

"Oh, yes." Eleanor got up clumsily, thanked the librarian, and started for home, carrying the printout in her hand.

And then, on the way back along Main Street, she

felt her bones stiffen with a purpose of steel.

Amanda Upshaw's party had been nothing. Who cared about a silly kids' party like that? *This* was the party she was meant to go to, the grand Concord celebration for Derek Alabaster.

She would go back to 1938 on Eddy's enchanted bike. She would find herself in the crowd around the great movie star. She would push forward until she was right beside him and whisper a warning in his ear, "Don't drive your car. Take the train."

She would save the life of the most famous movie star in history.

21

GONE AGAIN

*E*DDY WAS READY TO take off into the unknown.
Today was the day. He had decided to explore
ancient Rome in the days of Julius Caesar.

In his makeup Latin class he had asked a bold question. "If you could go back to ancient Rome, Mr. Orth,
what year would you choose?"

Somewhat to his surprise, Mr. Orth answered at
once. "I'd go back to 46 B.C., Caesar's triumphant entry
into Rome. There'd be a huge parade of Caesar's legions,
marching through the city with horns and drums, and
there'd be horses pulling chariots and defeated armies
in chains and maybe even elephants."

Eddy was charmed. "Elephants? Did you say elephants?"

"Well, probably elephants. Who knows? I'd love to go back and find out."

So that was settled. At home after school Eddy rushed upstairs to throw a few things into his backpack. He might need a sweater, and—what else? A flashlight. And what about his battery-powered radio? He'd play his radio for Julius Caesar and knock his socks off. Then it occurred to Eddy that there wouldn't be any broadcasting stations back there in ancient Rome, so he put new batteries in his tape recorder, deciding to take that instead.

Brilliant! Now he could bring home the actual sound of Caesar's army—the blaring horns, the trumpeting elephants, the clanking swords, the stamping horses, the thundering chariots, and Julius Caesar himself shouting, "I came, I saw, I conquered"—or words to that effect, only in Latin, of course.

But Eddy shouldn't have bothered. While he was upstairs, stuffing more and more things into the pouches and pockets of his backpack, his sister Eleanor was downstairs, home from the library, moving fast.

She marched straight down the hall to the corner under the stairs, threw aside the curtain, looked sharply at the Time Clock on the handlebars of the Time Bike, adjusted the dials with great care, and threw her leg over the crossbar.

Then, sitting down on the narrow saddle, she began to pedal furiously.

When Eddy dragged his backpack down the stairs, he was just in time to see the curtain flutter back and hang still. Horrified, he thrust his nose into the dark corner behind it.

The Time Bike was gone.

22

ELEANOR'S TURN

*T*UMBLING OFF THE BIKE, Eleanor heard the band. The thrilling noise came from the center of town. There were pounding drums and braying trombones and the deep gasping wheeze of Sousaphones—*BAH de BAH BAH, THUMPITY THUMP THUMP, BLOOPITY BLOOPITY BLOOP.*

Was she too late? Eleanor grasped the handlebars of the Time Bike and ran it down the hall, hardly glancing left and right, hardly noticing how different the house looked with its overstuffed furniture and dark pictures, recognizing the metal lady on the newel post, missing only the bust of Henry at the foot of the stairs.

It was hot, terribly hot. Eleanor was sorry to discover

that the Concord Town Party for Derek Alabaster had happened on one of those August days when the air wraps a damp blanket of heat around you, so you can hardly breathe. Oh, it was so hot. She took off her cotton jacket and folded it and stuffed it into the bicycle basket.

Where were all the people who lived at No. 40 Walden Street? Eleanor unhooked the screen door and nudged it open with the front wheel of the bike. Well, of course, they were all at the party. They must have followed the band to Monument Square.

But not their little dog. Eleanor gasped as a small furry creature darted past her, escaping from the house, yipping joyfully.

"Oh, no, little dog, you're not supposed to be out here." Eleanor leaned the bike against the wall of the house and tried to push him back inside.

He refused. He backed away, barking and yipping, and frolicked along the porch, looking back at her in doggy triumph. He bounced around a card table covered with papers. *"Yip, yip!"*

"Oh, well, never mind," said Eleanor. She brushed back her sticky hair and picked up the bike again.

It was dreadfully hot. The card table had been brought outside because the air was cooler out here. There was even a little breeze.

But whoever had been sitting at the table must have hurried away, because the chair beside the table was tipped over, as though the person had heard the band and jumped up and shouted, "Here they come," and then everyone had poured out of the house and rushed up the street and around the corner to Monument Square, and some of the papers had fluttered off the table and floated over the porch railing, and now they were still blowing around the front yard.

Eleanor lugged the bike down the porch steps, looking up in surprise at the elm trees along Walden Street. How beautiful they were, arching over the houses like green chandeliers.

Then she forgot the elm trees, because the noise of the band had stopped. The party had begun.

Quick, quick! Eleanor rushed the bike down the walk, with the little dog capering in front of her, jumping at the bike, bouncing at her legs, yipping and yapping.

"Oh, little dog, get out of the way," said Eleanor, because the welcoming speeches must have started already. Derek Alabaster, the greatest movie star in history, must be there in Monument Square right now.

Oh, hurry, hurry! Eleanor gripped the handlebars and rolled the clumsy bike toward the gate. She had to be in time to whisper her warning in Derek Alabaster's

107

ear and save his life.

But the tiny dog kept getting in the way. When one of the sheets of paper blew past her, the dog chased it, grasped it in his teeth, and bounced back to Eleanor.

She had to stop and take it from his itty-bitty jaws and pat him in congratulation, because he really was a funny little dog, even though there was no getting rid of him.

Carelessly she tossed the paper away, but the little dog thought it was a game, and he bounded after it, picked it up, and stood on his hind legs, offering it to Eleanor, wanting her to throw it so he could fetch it again, and then they could go on playing this wonderful game all afternoon.

"No, no," said Eleanor, "that's enough." This time she stuffed the paper under her folded jacket in the bicycle basket and walked firmly through the gate. Obediently the dog trotted after her, his little ears flopping up and down, his tiny paws scrambling to keep up.

There was no one else on Walden Street. Eleanor pushed the bike along the pavement as fast as she could, afraid to ride it for fear it would suddenly plunge forward or backward into some other time where she didn't want to be at all.

Awkwardly she steered it past the shops, surprised by the funny-looking cars parked on the street, and amazed to see the fire station right here in the middle of town, along with a vegetable market and a barber shop and a dime store. How strange and old-fashioned they looked!

At last, rounding the corner onto Main Street, Eleanor and the little dog joined a stream of other late-comers. The dog barked happily and cavorted in all directions, tripping up a man in a straw hat and a couple of little girls in pink dresses. The children squealed, their corkscrew curls bounced, and their mother shooed them ahead of her toward the sound of a familiar voice.

It was Derek Alabaster. It was Derek Alabaster himself. And instead of saying mean things to gorgeous Gloria Ruby, the way he was always doing in *Gone with the Storm*, he was thanking the selectmen of Concord for their speeches and the people of Concord for their welcome, and promising to sign all their autograph books.

There were cheers. Autograph books waggled in the air.

"Twenty minutes," cried Derek Alabaster. "I have twenty minutes before my next appointment. Come one, come all."

Only twenty minutes! Eleanor was dismayed. Around her the men and women of Concord in the year 1938 surged forward. The children of Concord were there too, big kids and little kids and babies in wicker buggies. Everybody was pushing past her, jamming into the throng around the Civil War monument, while the little dog yipped and tried to run between their legs.

Eleanor reached down with one arm, grabbed him by the collar, and dumped him in the basket. When she looked up again, Derek Alabaster had disappeared. Only the top of his head showed above the straw hats of the men and the permanent waves of the women.

It was just like the picture in the newspaper. Eleanor glanced around, and saw the photographer in the very act of taking the picture with his big camera.

She couldn't help laughing, wondering if she herself would be in it, along with the Time Bike and the little dog, even though they didn't belong in the Concord of 1938 at all. If she looked at that old paper again, would she see herself in the picture? But it was impossible. Well, of course, the whole thing was impossible.

And then, above the excited noises of the crowd, there was a sharp clear whistle. At once the little dog leaped joyfully out of the bicycle basket and disappeared between the legs of a short fat man in front of Eleanor. The man staggered and swore and turned around to glare at Eleanor and shout, "Is that your dog?"

"Not really," whispered Eleanor, snatching at the scrap of paper whisking out of the basket. Nimbly she caught it and stuffed it in the pocket of her jeans.

The grouchy man turned away and pushed forward with everybody else, part of the close-packed throng. Too many hopeful people were waving too many autograph books. Eleanor pushed forward too, and craned her neck, looking for the person who had whistled. It must have been a member of the family that lived at No. 40 Walden Street. Maybe it was Uncle Freddy's great-uncle, or his grandfather or grandmother.

There was too much thrust and bustle, too much shouting. And time was growing short. There were only a few minutes left to warn Derek Alabaster that *he must not drive away in his car.*

There it was, parked in front of the Town Hall, waiting for him, *the car of death.*

She struggled forward, jamming the front wheel of the Time Bike forward, using it as a wedge.

"Good gracious, child," said a red-faced woman in a big hat, fanning herself with her autograph book, "you shouldn't have brought that bicycle here."

"I'm sorry," said Eleanor, but she kept squeezing herself and the bike between the jostling men and women until she was only a few feet away from the great star of *Gone with the Storm.* But here she was completely blocked.

Too many hot sweaty bodies were crowded together

in a sweltering human wall. There was too much noise, too much commotion. They were all shouting questions, pushing their pieces of paper at the great star and brandishing their autograph books.

Eleanor felt sick. She pitied Derek Alabaster. With all those open mouths shouting for his attention and all those hungry faces staring at him in this awful heat, the poor man must be suffocating.

She backed away, pulling the bike to one side. By sidling back and around and still farther back and farther around, she made her way to the sidewalk in front of the Town Hall and approached Derek Alabaster's car.

The silver insignia on the radiator said Packard Super 8. It was the most beautiful automobile she had ever seen. It was twice as long as the boxy cars parked along Walden and Main, the old-fashioned Chevys and Pontiacs and Oldsmobiles.

A boy was sitting in the driver's seat, guarding the car, making sure no one made off with a piece of it—the radiator cap with its shiny little figure of Adonis, or the hubcaps, or the steering wheel, or anything else they could carry away as a souvenir.

He looked strangely familiar. When he smiled at Eleanor, he looked more familiar still.

"Oh, please," said Eleanor, "you mustn't let Mr. Alabaster drive this car."

The boy grinned and said, "Why not?"

"Because if he does, he'll die. There'll be a terrible wreck. Really and truly, there will be."

The boy laughed. "What are you, some kind of fortune-teller?"

"No," said Eleanor, and then she changed her mind. She looked at him earnestly. "Well, yes, in a way I am. I mean, I know what's going to happen, I really do. Oh, please, why can't he take the train?"

"It's funny," said the boy, and he leaned toward Eleanor as if telling her a secret. "I'm kind of worried myself. He's a terrible driver. Maybe I can persuade him to come with me." He gestured at the car behind the Packard Super 8. It was a small upright Model A Ford.

"Oh, yes," said Eleanor. "Yes, yes. Please make him go with you."

"Well, I don't know," said the boy. "He's pretty stubborn. Did you get his autograph?"

Eleanor shook her head. "I couldn't get anywhere near."

The boy flashed her a brilliant smile. "How'd you like mine?"

"Your autograph? Well, okay." Eleanor didn't want to hurt his feelings, so she took the piece of paper out of her pocket and looked at it. There was printing and writing on one side, but the other side was blank except for a few doggy toothmarks.

The boy produced a stubby pencil from somewhere, rested the paper on the dashboard, scribbled his name, and handed the paper back.

At once they were engulfed in a crowd of Derek Alabaster's fans. Eleanor had to back out of the way as they half carried, half pushed the greatest movie star of all time toward his car.

"No, no," cried Eleanor, "oh, please, no." She watched the boy with the flashing smile jump out of the driver's seat and put his face close to Alabaster's. He was gesturing at his own little Model A Ford.

Eleanor couldn't hear, but she could see the great movie star shake his head, push the boy aside, and sink grandly behind the wheel of his noble automobile. Tearfully she watched as the crowd moved out of the way, cheering and waving.

The engine *varoom*ed, and the car started forward. Eleanor burst into tears as it surged away and raced down Lexington Road.

Blindly she fumbled for the Time Bike. Sadly she rode it home.

23

HOME AGAIN

BACK IN THE HOUSE AT No. 40 Walden Street, Eleanor sat for a moment on the saddle of the bike as the whizzing wheels slowed down and the handlebars stopped trembling in her hands. For a moment she could hear a faint yipping, but then that faded too, as the little dog trotted back, back, back into history.

It was over. The excitement, the hero worship, the party, they were all over.

Eleanor sighed and stepped out into the old familiar front hall, with its desk and gooseneck lamp, its picture of a clipper ship on the wall beside the cuckoo clock, its plaster bust of Henry in the curve of the stairs, and the dusty velvet curtain hanging in the schoolroom door.

She was glad to be back, but she wished now that she had looked around more carefully at the house that had been here in 1938. She wished she had seen the ancestral faces of the people who had lived here then. She had met only one resident of No. 40 Walden Street, the little dog.

Still, it was a relief to belong here now, in this version of the house, to see one of the cats streak across the hall, to know that Uncle Freddy and Aunt Alex were here somewhere, and to be cool again, free of the clammy heat of that ancient August day.

And the tragedy was over. It had been over for more than sixty years. Slowly Eleanor climbed the stairs and went to her room to look at the photograph, the old picture the librarian had copied for her from the *Concord Journal* of August 16, 1938.

It was fuzzy and dim. She took it to the window and stared at it, then took off her glasses, rubbed them with her shirttail, put them back on, and looked again, trying to find the back of her own head in the crowd, her own pigtail, and perhaps a glimpse of the Time Bike between the elbows and hips and old-fashioned pocketbooks of the Concord fans of Derek Alabaster.

She couldn't find herself, nor could she find the bike. She couldn't even find the little dog, because he had been locked up in this very house before she had blundered back into his own time and unhooked the screen door and let him out.

It was all very mysterious.

24

Two Dangerous Visitors

ONCE AGAIN EDDY WAS ready to go. It was high time he had another turn with his own Time Bike.

So far his adventures had been unsatisfying. He had gone back two minutes (by accident), then forward a week (a disaster), then back one day (a mistake), and finally a long way back to the year 1817 (ridiculous). And then his stupid sister, Eleanor, had stolen the bike right out from under his nose.

So if he meant to be a true explorer of history, going and coming freely in the past and bringing back immensely important information, if he was ever going to change history's terrible blunders, it was time to begin.

Of course it was true that Eleanor had not been able to change history by saving the life of that dumb movie star when she stole Eddy's bike, but then Eleanor was not Eddy. She didn't think ahead, whereas he had studied and studied. He had read about Julius Caesar, he knew all about the Roman Forum. He was ready, his backpack was ready, the Time Bike was ready.

He had a last excited lunch with Aunt Alex and Uncle Freddy. Then, swallowing the final bite of his sandwich, he stood up and grinned at them, saying a secret farewell in his head. Then he put his plate and glass in the sink, *plink*, *plink*, saluted smartly, and marched out into the hall.

But at once he dodged back into the kitchen because it occurred to him to ask a question. What time was it right now? What time was it *exactly*? He needed to find out, because when he got back from his adventure he would ask again, and then he'd know how much *real* time had gone by while he was zooming back and forth in the *miraculous* time measured by the Time Clock. "What time does your wristwatch say, Uncle Freddy?"

His uncle pulled back his shirt cuff and looked at his watch. "Oh, I'm sorry, Eddy, it's run down. I forgot to wind it."

Then they all jumped at a squawk from the backyard, a noisy brag by the little rooster. At once Aunt Alex pulled off her apron and hurried outside with a basket, murmuring something about collecting eggs.

Eddy was exasperated. "Oh, Uncle Freddy, why don't you buy a quartz-crystal watch? How can you tell what time it is if you don't have a good watch?"

Uncle Freddy looked thoughtful, and then he stood up and said something ridiculous. "Maybe, Eddy, we could get along without clocks altogether. The world has its own rhythms. We could live by nature's clock."

"Oh, come on, Uncle Freddy."

"But we could, you know, Eddy. How do you think people got along before clocks were invented?"

"Not very well, I'll bet."

"Yes, they did. They understood the clock of the world. They got up in the morning with the crow of the cock, they planted crops by the progress of the stars." Uncle Freddy crooked his finger mysteriously, and said, "Come with me."

"Oh, Uncle Freddy," said Eddy, but he followed his uncle out to the front porch.

Uncle Freddy pointed at the sky, where the sun stood high over the roof of the house next door. "Tell me what time it is."

Eddy thought it over, trying to judge how far the sun had drifted away from the zenith. He made a wild guess. "Two o'clock?"

At that instant the cuckoo proclaimed noon, and the clock on the tower of the First Parish Church chimed twice.

"There," said Uncle Freddy, grinning in triumph, "you see?" He clapped Eddy on the back and went back in the kitchen to finish his coffee.

Eddy went indoors too, slamming the screen door behind him. The time had come. He was ready to go. And as he pulled aside the curtain under the stairs, he could see that his bike, too, was ready to go. Its headlight splashed a bright star on the wall. The wheel spokes glittered. The Time Clock hummed.

But then there was an interruption.

Briinnnngggggg! The doorbell was ringing, and someone was knocking on the front door with a sharp *rat-a-tat-tat.*

Uncle Freddy called from the kitchen, "See who it is, will you, Eddy?"

Briinnnnggggg! Briinnnnggggg! Briinnnnggggg! Rat-a-tat-tat!

Eddy poked his head out of the curtain under the stairs and saw a large shape on the other side of the oval glass of the front door, blotting out the light. "Oh, no," he said, dodging into the kitchen. "It's Mr. Preek."

Briinnnnggggg! Rat-a-tat! Briinnnnggggg!

"Oh, dear," said Uncle Freddy. He got up slowly

121

and went to the door.

Eddy disappeared upstairs to get his backpack and wait for the unwelcome visitor to go away. He could remember bad times with Mr. Preek in days gone by.

There were voices in the kitchen, loud braying remarks by Mr. Preek, murmurs from Uncle Freddy.

Eddy couldn't hear what they were saying—it was probably something to do with the Board of Selectmen. When the voices grew louder, he looked over the banister.

Oh, good, Mr. Preek was leaving. Eddy watched Uncle Freddy close the door softly and walk into the schoolroom, his shoulders drooping, his head down, staring at the floor.

But someone else was coming in the back door, looking up at Eddy, booming a cheerful hello.

It was Eddy's old friend Oliver Winslow. And this time it wasn't just a friendly visit.

"So okay," said Oliver as Eddy ran downstairs and dumped his backpack on the floor, "where is it?"

"Where is what?" said Eddy.

"Your bike. I mean, it sounds so really incredible. I just want to see how it works. Show me!"

25

THE BUCCANEER OF TIME

OLIVER WAS EDDY'S oldest friend. In eighth grade he had been the only kid six feet tall. He was a massive boy with powerful arms. It surely wasn't Oliver's fault that everything he touched came apart in his hands.

His mother would groan, "Oliver, dear, you don't know your own strength," when something else lay in ruins, a chair or a table or a pretty vase of flowers.

It was no wonder that last year he had wrecked the old Chevy Impala, the car everybody called the Green Horror. "You're just lucky you didn't break your fool neck," Oliver's father had said. The smashed car still sat behind the Winslows' house like a monument to Oliver's blundering clumsiness.

So it had been a terrible mistake on Eddy's part to tell him about the Time Bike, because today when Oliver walked into the house, he almost blew the place apart.

But at first he just said, "Show me!"

Eddy had a sinking feeling in his stomach, but what else could he do? Reluctantly he pointed at the curtain under the stairs.

"Oh, great, you mean it's right here?" Oliver grabbed the curtain and pulled it violently aside, ripping the crimson velvet.

"Oh, sorry," said Oliver, but he was staring at the Time Bike. "Hey, cool." At once he threw his massive leg over the crossbar and sat down heavily, squeezing the coiled springs under the seat.

They creaked and groaned. From the plastic clock on the wall came a warning squawk, as the cuckoo plunged out of his little door to tell the world it was time for bed.

"Hey, watch it, Oliver," said Eddy. "Come on, get off."

Oliver stayed put. His legs were too long for the pedals, but he put his ear to the Time Clock and said, "Hey, Eddy, listen to that, it's revving up. It's like I turned the key on my old Chevy. It's going *whah-whah-whah.* You hear that?"

"No," said Eddy. Reluctantly he explained how the mechanism worked, and then he tugged at Oliver's arm.

"Come on, Oliver, it's my bike. Get off."

"Hey, lookit," said Oliver, hardly listening. "The mirror—I can see things in it. Oh, wow, hey, Eddy, look at that. Headlights."

And then, to Eddy's horror, he took off.

"No, Oliver," cried Eddy, staring at the sudden emptiness of the dark corner under the stairs. "No, no." He snatched at the place where the handlebars had been, but they were gone.

There was only the trembling of the curtain and the faint tringling of a bicycle bell from far away, and another soft noise—*honk, honk*—what was that?

26

THE RETURN OF THE
GREEN HORROR

*I*T WAS THE WORST POSSIBLE thing that could have happened. Oliver Winslow was the very worst possible person to take the bike back in time. He was even worse than Hunky Poole.

What would Oliver do back there? He might blunder around and interfere with something really important. He might mess up the whole course of history.

Eddy wandered around the house feeling helpless and lost. He wanted to reach back into the past, whatever past it was, and yank Oliver out of there with his bare hands.

How could he have been so dumb? How could he

have told a crazy guy like Oliver about the Time Bike? What a mistake.

And of course Oliver *did* do something crazy with the Time Bike.

When he smashed his way back from his piratical spree into the past, Aunt Alex and Uncle Freddy were on their way to Boston to have dinner in a restaurant because it was Aunt Alex's birthday, Eleanor was in the kitchen making frosting for Aunt Alex's birthday cake, and Eddy was upstairs trying to do his algebra homework, thinking terrible thoughts instead.

But when the frightful noise began, Eleanor dropped her spoon and Eddy hurled himself downstairs, and together they rushed outside and stood gazing, thunderstruck, at the ghastly scene in the front yard.

Part of the picket fence was shattered, smashed by something that was erupting into view on the lawn. It was the crumpled front bumper and green hood of a car, a battered old Chevy Impala.

"It's the Green Horror," gasped Eleanor. Then she gave a small scream. Part of the chassis was coming into view with a clap of thunder.

"It's Oliver," shouted Eddy. "He's back."

There he was, Oliver Winslow, crouched in the front seat with his big hands gripping the steering wheel and his eyes squeezed shut. Then, with a noise like colliding locomotives, the buckled door of the backseat appeared, and then the trunk of the car and the rear wheels and the back bumper.

But that wasn't all. With a tumultuous blast like the roar of a cannon, something else emerged from the empty air.

It was the Time Bike. It was attached to the back of Oliver's car with fraying ropes and pieces of string. It shuddered and rattled, because the entire car was still shaking and clattering as it settled down, its metal skirts trembling and dropping specks of rust all over the grass.

At last the smashing and crashing stopped. Oliver opened his eyes and heaved open the car door. It was stuck, and he had to bash it open with his fist. Stepping out on the grass, he grinned at Eddy and Eleanor.

"Well, hi there," he said proudly. "Whaddaya know? I made it. Wanta take a ride?"

Eleanor's mind reeled. She started to laugh.

But it wasn't funny. Eddy charged down the porch steps, stumbling, nearly falling on his face. With clumsy fingers he untied the Time Bike and set his precious property down on the grass. Whatever nutty thing was going on, at least he had his bike back.

Carefully he leaned it against the porch steps. Only then did he turn around and yell at Oliver, "You stupid jerk, you're lucky to get back alive. You can't move cars around in time. Not a big thing like a car."

"Oh, can't I?" roared Oliver, and he slapped the crumpled hood of his ugly old Chevy Impala. "Well, what do you call this? Here it is, big as life."

But then it wasn't. The hood of the car disintegrated. There was a sighing sound like the wind in the trees, and the front of the car crumbled and disappeared. The greasy engine, with all its spark plugs and cylinders and hoses and fan belt, was gone.

Then the rest of Oliver's car evaporated, thinning to a greenish transparency, shimmering for an instant in the air, then vanishing altogether. Nothing was left in the front yard but the smashed fence and the flattened grass.

Eleanor laughed again, and couldn't stop.

Eddy laughed too, and clutched his bicycle, afraid that it too might disappear, but it didn't.

Oliver gaped at the volume of air that had once been occupied by his hideous machine. Then he grinned hugely and said, "Oh, well, what the heck." Bending down, he picked up something from the grass. "Well, looky here," he said, holding it out in the palm of his hand.

It was a spark plug, a memento of the Green Horror of days gone by. But then Eleanor whooped again as the spark plug faded too, leaving nothing in Oliver's big dirty hand.

Every bit of his old original Chevy Impala, snatched from the past and jammed into the present, was once again only a memory. Around the corner at Oliver's house the real Green Horror, a crumpled wreck, was alone in the world, its glory days over.

Eleanor calmed down and grinned at Oliver. "You know what? I made a cake. You want some?"

"Hey," said Eddy, "I thought it was for Aunt Alex."

"It's all right," said Eleanor. "I'll make another one."

"Well, okay." Eddy clapped Oliver on the back. Then he lifted his bike up the steps and set it down carefully in the front hall.

In the kitchen, still grinning, Eleanor swabbed icing on her cake and cut three big slabs. "Here you are, Oliver," she said, passing him a plate.

"Well, thanks," said Oliver, and he ate it greedily.

27

THE ENGINEERING GENIUS

"I KNEW SOMETHING WAS THE matter," said Aunt Alex, smiling at Uncle Freddy across the table in the restaurant. She was trying to be brave. "Thank you for telling me at last."

"Oh, my dear," said Uncle Freddy, "it's such a terrible birthday present."

"No, no, it's all right." Aunt Alex took a deep breath. "When are we going to tell the children?"

"Not till tomorrow, when I bring Georgie back from the lake. Then we can face it together."

"Of course." There was a quaver in Aunt Alex's voice. "Oh, it will be such an unhappy way to welcome her home." Then she brightened. "But we'll be so glad to have her back."

Aunt Alex was right. The other members of the family were pleased that Georgie was coming home, because everybody loved Georgie. But Eddy was not about to postpone his tremendous journey until tomorrow.

History was waiting for him. *Real* history.

His first attempt at going back into Henry Thoreau's time hadn't worked at all, so it didn't count. And Eleanor's silly adventure with the Time Bike had taken her back only a little way, just to see a movie star. So that didn't count either.

And he certainly couldn't count Oliver Winslow's crazy blundering into last year as a study of ancient history, because everybody in the world had been *alive* last year—well, everybody except newborn babies and dead people. Last year wasn't really *history*.

So if a serious research expedition into the past was ever going to happen, it was up to Edward P. Hall of No. 40 Walden Street in the town of Concord in the Commonwealth of Massachusetts at the beginning of the third millennium. The finger of destiny was pointing straight at Eddy.

But when Edward P. Hall strode down the front hall

to the special place behind the curtain under the stairs, meaning to set the clock of the Time Bike back more than two thousand years, he discovered something terrible.

It was broken. The top half of the Time Clock had pulled away from the bottom, and a spring was uncoiling through the crack.

It was Oliver's fault. Oliver always broke everything. He must have handled the bike roughly, forcing it to lug that enormous bulging heap of ugly metal back along the narrow corridor of time. No wonder the clock was broken. Now the delicate works would be all out of whack.

And what if some important part of the enchanted mechanism had already fallen out? What if pieces were lying all over the front yard?

Groaning, Eddy ran outside and began looking, just in case. At first he walked up and down, bent double, staring at blades of grass and tufts of clover and dandelions that had gone to seed, while the setting sun blazed across the front yard.

His back hurt, and he was hot and disgusted. He got down on hands and knees and crawled over the ground again, finding only a colony of ants in a hole and a tiny spider blowing off the end of a blade of grass, buoyed by a thread like a sail.

There was nothing on the lawn, no missing piece of the Time Clock. But at last Eddy found something in Aunt Alex's flowerbed, a small gear of shining brass nestled in a lily.

Exultant, he took it indoors and unscrewed the clock from its mounting on the handlebars. Then, leaving the screws and the screwdriver on the floor, he ran upstairs with the clock and the important little gear. In his bedroom he pushed his math homework out of the way and got to work.

An hour later, as the window darkened with evening and the cuckoo clock announced a silly hour in the middle of the night, all the parts of the Time Clock lay on a tray, along with Eddy's careful diagram showing exactly how everything fitted together—the wheel that counted years with its multitude of teeth, the day wheel with its hundreds of notches, the hairspring and escapement, the main spring, the gears and pinions, the spidery hands, and of course the little cogwheel he had found in the front yard.

It was disappointing that the clockworks seemed so ordinary. Eddy had hoped to find a beautiful jewel deep within the clock, a glowing crystal that was the secret of its amazing power. But there were only the usual gears and springs.

Putting everything back together would be no joke.

Eddy stared anxiously at the pieces on the tray. He was too hot to think.

He went looking for an electric fan. He found one in a closet, brought it back, set it on the table, plugged it in, switched it on, and sat down.

There, that was better. A little breeze ruffled Eddy's hair as he fitted the mechanism together again, tightening the coiled springs and trying the extra cogwheel in one place after another. At last he found a slot for it, and then there was nothing left to assemble but the white face of the clock and the two skinny hands. The broken pieces of glass stuck together somehow, and the job was done.

He was an engineering genius. Eddy stood up and stretched his arms over his head, feeling happy and proud. Carelessly he reached for the knob of the electric fan. But instead of switching it off, he turned it to high by mistake.

At once there was a rush of air like a hurricane. On the table the Time Clock rocked, and a shiny speck slid off onto the floor.

The door slammed downstairs. Aunt Alex called, "We're back!"

Eddy could hear Eleanor clattering down the stairs to show Aunt Alex her birthday cake—of course it was the *second* birthday cake, because Oliver Winslow had eaten most of the first one.

Eddy bent down to look under the table.

At first he saw nothing at all. He stood up and found his flashlight, then got down on his knees and pointed it this way and that. Almost at once he saw a sparkle in the corner. Delicately he picked it up between thumb and forefinger and looked at it.

The sparkling speck was a microscopic gear so small that the pinion was no thicker than a needle. Eddy thrust it into his pocket.

It couldn't be anything very important, because everything else fitted together so neatly. And it was so small.

As he galloped downstairs, the plastic clock on the wall struck a ridiculous hour—*Cuckoo! Cuckoo! Cuckoo!*

28

THE FINGER OF DESTINY

BUT OF COURSE HE WOULD have to wait till morning. Eddy was too hot and tired to begin anything as important as his great quest into history on a muggy night as dark as pitch. The Time Clock was fixed, the bike was ready to go, but the great time explorer himself was too sleepy to do anything but go to bed.

He meant to get up really early next morning, but he was awakened in the middle of the night by noises over his head. Uncle Freddy was up there in the attic again. Eddy listened until he heard his uncle come slowly down the attic stairs. By now he was wide awake. It took him hours to go back to sleep.

When he opened his eyes at last, sunlight was pouring into the room. Eddy leaped out of bed and threw on the same clothes he had worn yesterday.

When he ran downstairs for a hurried breakfast, Aunt Alex said, "Good morning, Eddy," and smiled at him brightly. "Uncle Freddy's on his way to New Hampshire to pick up Georgie. Won't it be lovely to see her again?"

"Oh, right, you bet." Eddy poured cereal into his bowl. "Good old Georgie." Then he looked up in surprise, and said, "What's that noise?"

"It's just Eleanor learning to drive." For a minute they sat listening as Aunt Alex's car bucked and jolted down the driveway with a grinding of gears and a screeching of brakes.

But soon Aunt Alex couldn't bear it. She jumped up to look out the window. "Oh, Eddy, do you think she's all right?"

"Who knows?" said Eddy, imagining another automotive disaster.

He gulped down his cereal in a hurry, eager to get going on a far more wonderful contraption than an ordinary everyday gasoline-driven four-cylinder ten-year-old secondhand car that might explode any minute.

But of course Eleanor didn't wreck Aunt Alex's car. In fact she was right there in the front hall, dangling the car keys in her hand, when he took off on the Time Bike.

Coming into the house, she caught a momentary glimpse of her brother as he thrust his foot down on the pedal of the bike and then—*poof!*—he was gone.

The corner under the stairs was empty. The curtain fluttered back and hung still.

29

STOP, STOP!

*E*DDY CAUGHT A BRIEF glimpse of his sister staring at him wildly. Her mouth was open, and the car keys were dropping from her hand. In the instant before everything at No. 40 Walden Street disappeared in the tumult of reversing time, she shouted something at him, but in the whistling rush of wind he couldn't hear, and anyway he had all he could do to hang on.

Bowing his head against the blast, Eddy gritted his teeth and told himself to hold tight and never let go, because a journey of two thousand years would take a long time.

When the bike began to slow down—too soon!—he thought something must be wrong. But the bike was only pausing; it didn't really stop. There was a flickering blur of old-fashioned shapes, people skittering backward, buggies backing up, and then with a sickening lurch the bike bounded forward at full speed. Almost at once there was a terrible clatter, and it rattled to a stop.

What had happened? Was something broken? Glancing down at the front wheel, Eddy saw a stick jammed into the spokes. He jerked it out and looked up into the thunderstruck face of a half-naked man. The stick was an arrow, just fired from his bow. At once the Time Bike lurched into motion again, and Eddy heard only the faint crashing of some large animal getting away.

After that there were a few more pauses, glimpses of tall trees shrinking into saplings, and then again the blur of passing centuries, and once in a while flashes of forests thickening and disappearing and coming back. Forests, nothing but forests!

Crouched on the seat of his plunging bicycle, Eddy had an unhappy thought. Even if the bike took him all the way back to the right time, he'd be in the wrong part of the world. These woods and trees were *American* woods and trees. He would *still* be at No. 40 Walden Street in Concord, Massachusetts, back when it was a wild and untamed wilderness.

He wouldn't be in ancient Italy at all, he wouldn't see

the Roman Forum and all those people wearing white robes and going in and out of marble temples.

With a sinking heart Eddy bent lower over the handlebars, feeling a change in the motion of the Time Bike. Now it seemed to be hammering against barriers, ramming its way through time, smashing the glass walls between centuries. Shards of days and splinters of years whistled past him. Whole fragments of the shattered calendar flew up in front of the bike.

And it was taking too long. "Stop," whispered Eddy, "please, stop." But the bike only surged onward faster and faster, whining and jolting and careening, whirling into bottomless gulfs of history, tumbling backward in plunges of a thousand years at a time.

What if it never stopped? What if it carried him back to the molten earth at its very beginning, or even further back to a time before the solar system was born? What if he found himself drifting in the darkness and absolute zero of interstellar space? "Stop," cried Eddy. "Stop, stop!"

But the bike would not stop. Eddy crouched low, remembering with homesick longing the warm kitchen at No. 40 Walden Street in that remote future time to which he might never return. Tears streaked past his ears, and he shouted again, *"STOP! I SAID, STOP!"*

It was no good. The Time Bike would never stop

unless he forced it to stop. In desperation Eddy thought of a dangerous, crazy thing to do. He jerked on the handlebars, bucked the front wheel up, skidded on the back wheel, and threw himself down, slamming the bike over on its side.

It fell with a sharp explosive crack and slid heavily along the ground, its wheels madly whirling, dragging Eddy with it, until at last it shuddered to a stop.

For a while he lay still with his eyes closed, sprawled under the bike with one leg tangled in the chain and his hurt side throbbing. But he was relieved and glad. The hurtling rush into nothingness had come to an end. He had come down in one time and one place, and he didn't care when it was or where.

A little breeze fanned his hair. He could feel the sun on his cheek. Opening his eyes, Eddy saw sky overhead, bright and blue. The wheels of the bike were still whirling. He pulled his legs clear and staggered to his feet.

Where was he? Was this place really the ancient prehistoric beginning of No. 40 Walden Street? Had the big homely house that Eddy had grown up in, with all its rickety porches and its funny-looking tower and plaster busts and attic and cellar, had that whole entire heap of splintery boards and curling shingles and windows and gables sprung up in this very place thousands of years later?

The place was a beach, a long stretch of sand with a rocky bluff on one side and the sea on the other. Waves purled up on the beach and flowed back. From the endless reach of seashore stretching left and right rose a murmur that he had heard before.

It had come from the bike itself, and from the clock on the handlebars. Sometimes the clock made a buzzing noise, sometimes it crowed like a cock, and sometimes it made this soft sound of water moving gently in and out.

It was a lovely landscape, this ancient shore with its white sandy beach and rocky headlands, but Eddy had no intention of staying. He was not going to swim in the surf or climb the bluff or explore the beach. He had to get back.

Now that he had at last stopped at a real place in a real time, he could simply set the clock forward and race through all those thousands of years until he came back to the era when the village of Concord would begin emerging from the forest. First there would be the wigwams of the Indians and then the simple houses of the English settlers. And at last his own ugly house at No. 40 Walden would spring up in a clutter of lumber, and he'd be home again in his own comfortable century.

He picked up the bike. It was in bad shape. The fenders were dented, the pedals were gritty with sand, and pebbles were wedged in the links of the chain and the spokes of the wheels. But the frame wasn't bent, the wheels turned freely, and the handlebars were securely attached to the fork.

Then Eddy was dismayed to see that the mounting for the Time Clock was empty. With a cry, he fell to his knees. The clock lay on the sand, broken again and burst apart. This time the glass was completely shattered, the springs were uncoiled in all directions, the escapement was bent and the balance wheel broken. The spidery hands were snapped in two.

And then, to his horror, Eddy saw a little wave curl around a heap of scattered gears and pull them away.

"Wait, wait!" Eddy splashed into the wave as it carried them out into deeper water. For a moment they floated, winking in the sunlight, and his frantic fingers snatched up one. The others sank and were swept out to sea.

With the tide sucking heavily at his legs and a turmoil of sand foaming around his ankles, Eddy struggled backward. When he staggered up the beach to the place where his bike stood, leaning on its kickstand, he grasped it and dragged it higher up the sloping sand to the bottom of the rocky bluff, to a flat-topped boulder like a table.

Sinking down, he leaned his back against the boulder

and pulled off his drenched sneakers.

Then, grief-stricken, he gazed at the blank blue surface of the Atlantic as it washed in and out over the place where thousands of years from now his own house would stand, high and strange, with all its eccentric porches and its oriental tower and its well-loved indoor spaces.

How would he get back? How was he ever going to get back?

30

STUCK!

WHY DID THINGS ALWAYS go wrong? Eddy looked wretchedly at the Time Bike. Maybe it was a present from the devil, not Prince Krishna, that generous giver of so many good things.

But Eddy didn't believe in the devil. Grimly he set to work cleaning pebbles out of the wheel spokes and the links of the chain.

Of course he knew perfectly well what had gone wrong. It was his own stupid fault. Like a moron he had repaired the Time Clock without bothering to find a place for the most precious piece of all.

Miserably Eddy felt in his pants pocket for the tiny leftover gear and looked at it on the palm of his hand.

The miniature brass wheel glittered in the sunlight. It must surely be the guiding intelligence, the immensely important key to the goings and comings of the Time Bike. Without this little gear there was no direction. The bike had not known when to stop, and Eddy had been forced to stop it himself with a violence that had smashed the delicate clock that was his only hope of getting home.

Heartsick, he put the gear back in his pocket and looked up and down the beach. On either side the shore stretched into the blue distance, headland beyond headland. Would he be stuck here for the rest of his life?

How would he live? He was hungry already.

Behind him on the landward side, somewhere over there beyond the crest of the bluff, he could hear a familiar sound, the soft chatter of wildfowl like the clucking of Aunt Alex's little hens. Gloomily he imagined wringing the neck of a chicken. Maybe he could be another Robinson Crusoe and live by hunting and fishing.

"I'll just go home for a frying pan," he joked to himself, "and a box of matches."

But it wasn't funny. Eddy despaired. Oh, sure, once upon a time he might have liked the idea of a free wild life, striding around a desert island under a palm-leaf parasol. But for Robinson Crusoe there had been a wrecked ship to plunder. Crusoe had rescued all sorts of tools from the ship—a gun and a knife and a shovel, and probably a tinderbox or a flint for lighting a fire.

Eddy had nothing.

He couldn't bear it. He jumped up with tears in his eyes and strode down to the edge of the water. For a while he walked doggedly along the hard wet sand, head down, pretending to look for shells, remembering a happy summer day at Crane's Beach.

They had come home sunburned and sandy with their pockets full of stones and shells. Eddy remembered Aunt Alex's collection of beach glass, pretty green fragments of bottles ground down by the sea.

There were no ground-up bottles on this ancient beach, but there were plenty of shells. Eddy almost forgot his misery as he picked up shell after shell. Then he found one so big and fine, he threw the others away and carried it back to the place where he had left his bike. He dropped the shell in the basket and sat down again on the sand beside the big flat rock.

His tears began again. For a long time Eddy sat huddled under the brow of the cliff, rocking back and forth on his bony haunches with his arms wrapped tightly around his knees.

There was no one to hear him, no one to help. The only sound beyond his gulping sobs was the sighing

149

whisper of the tide as it breathed in and out, sending waves the color of pearls gliding up on the sand and drawing them back.

There was no sail on the horizon, not even some rough craft hollowed out of a log. There was no other human being in the whole world. Eddy longed to see someone, anyone, even some boring person, the most boring person he had ever met. He imagined a figure walking primly along the sand—Miss Brisket, his social studies teacher, for instance. "Oh, Miss Brisket," he would shout, running to greet her, waving his arms in welcome.

But of course there was no one. Eddy tried to pull himself together. Wiping his nose on his sleeve, he looked around. The sun had set, and a few stars were shining in the sky. Over his head there was a familiar rush of wings.

He looked up to see a flock of wild geese racing in a line along the shore, their feathery breasts rosy in the light of the setting sun. They were shouting, *a-WARK! a-WARK!*

It was the same urgent cry that rang out over the town of Concord whenever their distant descendants flew over the rooftops in the spring and the fall. It made Eddy more homesick than ever.

His stomach growled with hunger. And something

was grinding into his hipbone. He took the little cog-wheel out of his pocket again and looked at it bitterly. It was so small and yet at the same time so powerful.

Then Eddy had half a thought—no, a quarter of a thought, the tiniest fraction of an idea. He held the little gear between middle finger and thumb and spun it with an expert twist and dropped it on the flat surface of the rock.

It behaved like a perfect top. For a moment it spun gaily around and around before slowing down and tipping over and rolling in a little circle. Eddy felt dizzy, as though he too had been spinning. He looked up. Had something happened? He was just in time to catch the horizon jerking slyly to a stop.

Once again he spun the little wheel, throwing his whole wrist into it this time, and watched as it whirled and hopped and danced. And this time he saw the landscape dance and spin like the top, whirling and whirling around him, the whole sea, the whole beach, the whole sky!

Giddily, Eddy begged the top to keep going, to keep spinning, to whirl him away, to take him home. But it didn't, it wouldn't. Once again the little gear danced more and more slowly, and at last it fell over, and the spinning ocean and circling sky slowed down and rocked to a stop.

It wasn't enough. The top alone was not enough. It needed something more.

Eddy threw himself down and lay on his back and stared up at the darkening sky, where a million stars were shining. It was astonishing to see them, because they didn't shine like that at home. The glow from a million lamps in the city of Boston blotted most of them out.

He turned on his side and saw the planet Venus, good old Venus, dropping toward the horizon after the sun, following its own natural law like a ball on a string.

The stars too were arching across the sky just as they did in his own time, moving like clockwork. The moon was obedient too. Above the planet Venus, Eddy could see its skinny crescent poised like a scraping of lemon rind. He closed his eyes and listened to the quiet pulse of the surf.

And then another ghost of a thought came to him. It couldn't be called an idea. There wasn't enough to put into words. It was just a memory of something Uncle Freddy had said.

He had been talking about natural time. His watch had stopped, but Uncle Freddy had said it didn't matter, because nature's clock never ran down. He had told Eddy right there on the front porch, "We could live by nature's clock."

Eddy stood up slowly and looked at his bike. It was standing at an angle, glistening a little in the starlight. The headlight sparkled, the reflector on the rear fender was red and bright. And the bike was shivering in its old eager way, ready to take off.

Then Eddy laughed, because there was a piercing screech somewhere behind him from the rooster that was master of the flock of wild hens. The rooster's crow was a talisman, it was part of nature's timetable, and so was the sun, which was rising now somewhere on the other side of the world. The tops of high mountains in Nepal were lighting up, and everywhere all over the earth the tides were rolling in on rocky shores and shallow bays in answer to the pull of the moon. And the wild geese were shouting, *"Spring now! Fall now!"* because nature's rhythms were never wrong. They were always right, like a clock that never needs winding, a clock that never runs down.

For the last time Eddy picked up the little notched gear that was connected in some mysterious way with universal time, and flung it down with the strongest twist in the power of his clever fingers.

Never had a top been spun so well. This time it bounded and rollicked joyfully, and jigged and galloped and reeled as if it would never stop. And of course it must never stop. It must never, never stop.

Calmly Eddy picked up his bicycle and mounted the high seat and leaned forward to tell the bike what to do. It was a kind of charm or incantation: "By the rooster's crow and the beat of my heart, by high tide and low tide and springtime and fall, by star-rise and moonset and darkness and dawn, by the clock of the world, dear bike, take me home."

31

THE MISSING DEED

ONCE AGAIN THE BIKE was back in its old nest
under the stairs, in the shadowy place behind
the curtain. For a moment Eddy heard the whisper of incoming and outgoing waves and the cry of the
wild geese, but then they faded away and were gone, all
gone except for the noisy crow of the rooster, *"ARK-
ARK-ARK-AROOOOOO."*

Then Eddy grinned and corrected himself, because
it wasn't the rooster of thousands of years ago, it was a
twenty-first-century rooster, alive and well right here
and now. It was Aunt Alex's Black Rosecomb bantam
cock with its shining black feathers and flaunting green
tail, proclaiming its kingship over the hen yard.

Eddy was home again for sure. His trembling hands fell from the handlebars; he slumped on the narrow saddle and hung his head. His bare feet slipped from the pedals and thudded on the floor.

The bike seemed tired too. It shivered and shook. Slowing down, the front wheel rattled against the twisted fender.

He sat for a minute with his eyes closed, basking in the afternoon sounds of the household—the drone of Eleanor's sewing machine, the clash of Aunt Alex's pots and pans, the wheezing squawk of the plastic cuckoo, and the slam of the screen door.

Eddy gave the shuddering handlebars a pat of thanks and stepped out into the hall.

Aunt Alex was there, running out of the kitchen, clapping her hands, and Eleanor was plunging down the stairs, because Uncle Freddy was back from Squam Lake with Georgie.

There she was, gangly little Georgie, beaming with delight, holding a jar of pollywogs and a turtle in a box.

"What's your turtle's name, Georgie?" said Eddy, the lordly big stepcousin, peering into the box.

"Oh," said Georgie, stricken. "I don't know." She stared at the turtle and tried to think. It was black, with a grave reptile face. It didn't look like a person with a name. It looked like what it was, a wild creature. Soon she would let it go in Walden Pond.

Uncle Freddy was pale and tired from his long drive. Over Georgie's head he looked gravely at Aunt Alex.

She shook her head and said softly, "After supper."

It was a festive meal. Aunt Alex spooned mashed potatoes onto everyone's plate, and Uncle Freddy carved the roast chicken. Of course the chicken came from the grocery store, because Aunt Alex would never have cooked one of her own little bantam hens.

Dessert was her own leftover birthday cake. "Do you like it, Georgie?" said Eleanor proudly. "Guess who made it."

"You did," said Georgie. *"Mmm-mmm."*

At last Aunt Alex pushed back her chair, Eleanor gathered up the plates, and Eddy patted his stomach and belched politely as a compliment to his sister.

Aunt Alex looked at him in surprise, Eleanor gave him a poke, and Georgie giggled.

Uncle Freddy stood up and looked at them soberly. "I'm afraid . . ." he began, and then he faltered and sank down in his chair as if he couldn't go on.

So it was up to Aunt Alex to tell the bad news. "We have to give up the house," she said quietly. "It does not belong to us."

Eleanor, Eddy, and Georgie stared at her in disbelief. "But we've always lived here," protested Eleanor. "I mean, it's *our house*."

"It's *always* been our house," said Eddy.

Georgie looked timidly at her mother and said nothing.

Uncle Freddy sighed. "It turns out that my parents never had a deed to the property. They seem to have taken it over in 1938 without any legal papers at all."

"But who did they take it *from*?" said Eleanor. "Who did it belong to before?"

There was an uncomfortable pause, and then Aunt Alex said softly, "Do you remember Miss Prawn?"

"Miss Prawn!" Eddy and Eleanor gasped with horror. They remembered their awful neighbor all too well. They had been so glad when she had moved away!

Georgie too remembered Miss Prawn, and her eyes widened in dismay.

"You mean our house really belongs to *Miss Prawn*?" cried Eddy.

Uncle Freddy tried to sound calm. "I'm afraid so. Mr. Preek tells me that it was the property of Miss Prawn's uncle, and he was an old bachelor, so when he died, my mother and father just moved right in. They didn't pay for it, Mr. Preek says. They just took it."

"But they couldn't have," said Eddy, dumbfounded. "They never would have done a thing like that, would they, Uncle Freddy?"

"The trouble is," said Aunt Alex, "there isn't any paper to prove they bought it fair and square. There's no deed." Trying to keep her voice steady, she went on, "Now don't worry. It only means we'll have to find another place to live. Something inexpensive, of course, something small."

"And we won't be able to afford Concord anymore, I'm afraid," said Uncle Freddy sadly.

Georgie's eyes filled with tears. Eddy was aghast. "Not live in Concord?"

"Oh, Eddy, dear," said Aunt Alex, nearly breaking down, "there are plenty of other nice towns to live in."

"But . . ." said Eddy. He was too stupefied to put his feelings into words.

Then Eleanor spoke up dreamily. "Tell me, Uncle Freddy, what does a deed look like?"

"Oh, Eleanor, I don't know exactly." Uncle Freddy stared at the ceiling, trying to think. "It's a document of some sort, and it probably says 'Quitclaim Deed,' or something like that, with words about 'a certain parcel of land with the buildings thereon'—that sort of language, I think." Sorrowfully he put his head in his hands. "I've looked for it everywhere. It's nowhere in the house. It's not in the attic. It's not anywhere at all. I'm very much afraid Mr. Preek is right."

Eleanor stood up. "Just a minute," she said softly.

"I'll be right back."

And when she returned to the kitchen a moment later, the missing deed was in her hand.

There it was, the rumpled scrap of paper that had been blowing across the front yard of this very house back in 1938, the same wrinkled document that had been seized by the little dog, the self-same piece of paper she had taken from his teeth and dropped in the basket of the Time Bike, the identical grubby certificate that had been autographed on the other side by Derek Alabaster's young friend and assistant, the boy behind the wheel of the Packard Super 8.

Eleanor put the paper down tenderly on the kitchen table and said, "Is this what you were looking for, Uncle Freddy?"

And of course it was. Uncle Freddy snatched it up with a glad cry, Aunt Alex burst into tears, Georgie ran happily out of the kitchen with a crumb of cake for her turtle, and Eddy looked at Eleanor with a knowing grin.

She knew what he was thinking, and she thought so too—in spite of all their mistakes and disasters, the Time Bike had been good for something after all. And somehow, although Oliver's crazy car, the Green Horror, had vanished into thin air after its astonishing return from last year, in *spite* of that fact, the marvelous quit-claim deed, proclaiming that a certain parcel of land was the property of Uncle Freddy's direct ancestor, had remained safely in Eleanor's pocket all the time. It had not disappeared.

Why not? Well, it was simple, really. Eleanor figured it out. The wonderful deed was only a single piece of paper, not two, whereas Oliver's car from last year had tried to crash its way into a world that already contained a Green Horror, and that had been impossible.

Not till later on, not till after the rejoicing was over and the hugging and dancing up and down and the slappings on the back, not till Aunt Alex said, "Oh!" and opened the refrigerator door to pull out a bottle and say, "I knew there was champagne in here somewhere," not till then did Eleanor take the paper back from Uncle Freddy and turn it over to see the signature on the back.

It was another miracle. She smiled to herself and smoothed the precious wrinkled sheet. She had failed to get the autograph she wanted, the signature of Derek Alabaster, but on the back of the deed to No. 40 Walden Street there was another wonderful name in bold handwriting.

The boy who had scribbled his autograph on the back of the deed to No. 40 Walden Street was none other than Gary Stewart! Gary Stewart himself! He must have been a young beginning actor back in 1938, but even then he had guessed what a famous heartthrob he was going to be, he had known what a superstar he was about to become.

Eleanor showed the signature to Eddy, and he had to admit he was impressed. "Gary Stewart! You saw Gary Stewart in person? Wow."

32

A Ship on the Seas
of Time

T HE NEXT TIME SOMEONE came to the front door, it was Oliver Winslow.

Georgie was skipping rope in the front hall beside the bust of Henry Thoreau. She kept on jumping, but she smiled at Oliver as she bounced up and down, her feet pattering lightly on the floor.

"My mom wants a dozen eggs, okay?" said Oliver, looking through the bulge of the screen. "Hey, is Eddy home?"

One of the cats sauntered out of the parlor, followed by Eleanor. "He was here a minute ago," said Eleanor. She shouted, "Eddy? Hey, Eddy!"

"Ninety-nine, a hundred," gasped Georgie, and stopped jumping.

"Well, come on in, Oliver," said Eleanor. "The eggs are in the kitchen."

Another cat skittered down the stairs. "Oh, hi there, Oliver," said Eddy, thundering down after the cat.

"Hey, Eddy," said Oliver. "There's this incredible new TV series, and it's really fabulous. Like there's this astronaut and he takes off in a spacecraft and then the whole entire world blows up. Oh, hi, Mrs. Hall. My mom wants a dozen eggs."

A lot of people straggled out of the schoolroom, talking and laughing—Uncle Freddy's students with their notebooks under their arms. They said hello and goodbye to Eddy and Eleanor and Aunt Alex and Georgie, and then Arthur Hathaway stepped on one of the cats.

It yowled. The screen door banged. Uncle Freddy emerged from the schoolroom with his lecture notes and said hello to Oliver.

Aunt Alex and Oliver disappeared into the kitchen, Georgie ran outdoors, Eleanor whisked past Eddy and hurried upstairs, and Uncle Freddy left the house to walk up the street to a meeting with the other selectmen.

Eddy was left alone in the front hall—alone if you didn't count the plaster bust of Henry at the foot of the stairs and the metal figure of Mrs. Truth on the newel post.

Gently he pulled aside the curtain and looked at the Time Bike.

Its travels were over. The clock that had guided it forward and backward through time was lying in smithereens on the sand of an ancient shore, and some of its precious gears had washed out to sea.

The rocket-shaped headlight still shone bravely on the wall of the coat closet, but the rims of the wheels were encrusted with prehistoric sand, and so was the wicker basket.

Idly, Eddy reached into the basket and took out the shell he had picked up on the beach.

It was the kind called a chambered nautilus, and something twanged in his brain, a wisp of a memory from the old days when the diamond in the attic window had done such astonishing things—hadn't there been something about "a ship of pearl"?

Well, that was all over now. And this was over too. Eddy took the shell into the parlor, set it down on the mantelpiece, and went looking for Oliver Winslow.

The makeup classes in the Sanborn School were over. And so for the rest of the summer Eddy and Eleanor lived from moment to moment, enjoying the here and now. But they couldn't help noticing that their summer with the Time Bike had some peculiar consequences.

The first was the loss of Eddy's sneakers. Two large shoes, bought in Concord at the beginning of the third millennium by a young Concord citizen with very large feet, had been left on a sandy shore in a remote era in the distant past.

"I'm sorry, Aunt Alex," said Eddy. "Look, I'm busting out of last year's sneakers." He held up one foot to show her the way his toes stuck out of the holes.

Aunt Alex looked up from her typewriter. She was puzzled. "But what happened to your new sneakers, Eddy dear?"

"I don't know," said Eddy. "I'm afraid they're gone for good."

So Aunt Alex drove him to Lexington for a huge new pair of shoes.

A second item on the list was the change in Amanda Upshaw. One Saturday afternoon Eleanor nearly collided with her on Main Street. Amanda was coming out of a dress shop carrying a pink paper bag. Eleanor smiled and said, "Well, hello there, Amanda."

Amanda looked at her in surprise. Eleanor Hall looked different somehow, really so incredibly different. "I'm having some kids over this afternoon," said

Amanda. "Want to come?"

"Oh, no, I'm sorry," said Eleanor, starting across the street. "I can't come today."

Nor any other day. So sorry, Amanda.

The third thing was a sharp crash one day as the cuckoo clock fell off the wall and smashed on the floor just as Eddy galloped by, thumping heavily in his new shoes. He stopped short in dismay and watched as the little plastic bird wobbled on its spring and croaked a last dying *"Cuckoo"*—the wrong time, as usual.

Aunt Alex ran out of the schoolroom and saw the shattered pieces on the floor.

"I didn't touch it, Aunt Alex," said Eddy, "ab-so-lute-ly not," and he burst out laughing.

Aunt Alex laughed too. Eleanor ran down the stairs to see what was happening, and she too was convulsed. So was Uncle Freddy, coming out of the kitchen. Georgie wasn't sure what was funny, but she laughed with everybody else.

"Well, it was a cuckoo cuckoo clock, anyway," said Eddy, picking up the pieces.

The fourth thing was an amazing remark by a scientific friend of Uncle Freddy's.

One day the friend noticed the shell on the mantelpiece, the chambered nautilus Eddy had brought back from that ancient seashore. "How interesting," he said, "an extinct example of the suborder *Tetrabranchiata Nautiloidea.* How on earth did you find one in such perfect condition?"

Uncle Freddy shook his head. He had no idea.

The fifth thing was the amazing relighting of Mrs. Truth's star-shaped lamp.

Soon after Eddy's bicycle came plunging home from the faraway past, he noticed that the bulb in the rocket-shaped headlight was at last growing dim, and he gave it an encouraging whack.

At once it sputtered out, but at the same instant, to his flabbergasted surprise, the light flared up in the glassy star held high in the hand of Mrs. Truth.

After that, of course, the front hall was no longer gloomy and dark. It was lit by some sort of blazing thousand-watt bulb. Every part of the hall was now exposed in all its dinginess.

Aunt Alex was startled to see the dust under the umbrella stand and the greasy fingermarks on the kitchen door. She told herself that she would clean the house very soon—well, as soon as her lectures were ready for the fall.

But of course she wouldn't polish away the new stains on the bronze skirts of Mrs. Truth, because they looked like pictures. There was a blotch like a bicycle and another like a rooster, and all down one side of her long metal gown a scattering of spots like little wheels and gears.

There was a sixth new thing that was impossible to explain. Neither Eddy nor Eleanor could have put it into words, but for both of them something in the air had changed. And not just in the air, but in the house too. It flowed along the Mill Brook across the street, and rustled in the trees, and shone in the sun, moon, and stars. From now on and forever after, Eleanor would be standing in a narrow crack in time, and Eddy too—one foot in the past and the other in the future. The thing that everyone called NOW, this quick passing moment right HERE, right NOW, was only a speck, a snap of the fingers, and yet it was also something more enormous and vast.

"Eddy," said Uncle Freddy, one day in the middle of August, "if you're not going to ride your bicycle anymore, could you put it somewhere else? Aunt Alex and I could use that corner under the stairs for our file cabinets. There's no space left in the schoolroom."

So the Time Bike was removed to a permanent safe home in the attic—Eddy's wonderful bicycle that had transported Eleanor to the Concord of sixty years ago and carried Eddy himself a little way into the future and far, far back into the past.

Prince Krishna's gift, the Time Bike, was mothballed like a battleship after a war.

Eddy lifted it up the two flights of stairs, trying not to run into railings and doorframes, bumping into them just the same, knocking chips of paint off the wood-work. In the attic he set it reverently down in the middle of the floor next to the snowflake wedding gown, and right behind the box in which the old American flag had been so carefully laid away.

When he came loping downstairs again, Aunt Alex was sitting at her desk in the hall with a pen in her hand. She looked up at Eddy and said, "I'm writing to Prince Krishna and your aunt Lily. Do you want to add any-thing, Eddy dear?"

He paused halfway down the stairs and said, "Just give them my love, Aunt Alex." Then he jumped down the six remaining steps, skidded on the rug, and crashed into the radiator.

So their adventures in time were over. Or were they? Surely the old house at No. 40 Walden Street was some-thing like a Time Machine itself? The future flowed into it through every crack and crevice and window and door, and the present snapped and crackled inside, as the five members of the family tumbled around from room to room, carrying on their daily lives, and then at last the ribbon of time unrolled up the stairs to store away the past in the hollow spaces of the attic.

If you were to walk along Walden Street past No. 40 and glance up at its funny tower and Victorian porches, you'd never think it was a monument to the flow of time. And yet it was.

Or perhaps—Eddy had a dream about it one night— perhaps the house was a high creaking ship pitching forward and wallowing in the seas of time, its sails ballooning from chimney and attic, from porch and tower, while Aunt Alex's chickens clucked on the quarterdeck and the cats meowed in the rigging and the rooster crowed from the maintop, and a handsome figurehead lighted the way with her outstretched lamp, and Henry stood staunchly at the wheel, his plaster hair tossing in the breeze.

The front porch, of course, was the bow of the ship, and there they all stood, Uncle Freddy and Aunt Alex and Georgie and Eleanor and Eddy, leaning over the railing, peering into the mists of time.

"What do you see?" shouted Eddy.

"Nothing," bawled Uncle Freddy.

"It's too foggy out there," squealed Georgie.

"I can't make out a thing," cried Aunt Alex.

"You can't see your hand in front of your face," screamed Eleanor.

But on the peak of the topmast the rooster, who could see farther than anybody, crowed, *"ARK-ARK-AROOOOOO!"*